The
Backyard Ghost

The
Backyard Ghost

by Lynn Cullen

For Janelle—
Your grandkids are very lucky. I hope they enjoy the book.
Lynn Cullen
6/22/93

CLARION BOOKS • NEW YORK

Friday the 13th Party Invitation by Lauren Cullen

Clarion Books
a Houghton Mifflin Company imprint
215 Park Avenue South, New York, NY 10003
Text copyright © 1993 by Lynn Cullen

Library of Congress Cataloging-in-Publication Data

Cullen, Lynn.
The backyard ghost / by Lynn Cullen.
p.   cm.
Summary: Eleanor's desperate attempts to break into the popular
crowd at her new school are complicated by her discovery that her
back yard is haunted by a Civil War ghost.
ISBN 0-395-64527-1
[1. Ghosts—Fiction.   2. Friendship—Fiction.   3. Popularity—
Fiction.   4. Schools—Fiction.]   I. Title.
PZ7.C8963Bac   1993
[Fic]—dc20   92-24580
                                                           CIP
                                                            AC
BP   10   9   8   7   6   5   4   3   2   1

For my father, William E. Doughty,
with love

Contents

The
Backyard Ghost

⟦ 1 ⟧

Popularity—How to Get It

Eleanor Cotton hurried across her backyard. The lot sloped down to a weedy pond, but Eleanor stopped short of the water. At the huge old oak, she paused to look over her shoulder. No one was coming. Good. She chose a tree root and sat down. The gnarled old root made a lumpy seat, but Eleanor didn't care. She had escaped them all—her nosy seven-year-old sister, Audrey; her mom; her dad; her brother, Ben. It was late Thursday afternoon, and she had the yard to herself. Furtively, she spread open the magazine she had rolled up in her fist.

Finding the magazine had been like a miracle. One minute Eleanor had been standing in line at Kroger's, pestering her mom for a Kit Kat bar, and the next minute she had seen the answer to all her problems.

It wasn't the main headline, which screamed in large black print THREE-YEAR-OLD GIVES BIRTH TO SIX-

1

POUND GIRL, that made Eleanor catch her breath. It was a smaller headline, near the bottom of the page. POPULARITY, it read. WHO'S GOT IT—HOW TO GET IT.

Eleanor didn't have it. Eleanor wanted to get it.

It took ninety-five cents of her allowance money and a promise to run the vacuum cleaner in all the bedrooms, but Eleanor got her magazine. Now, as she settled herself atop the bumpy root, she could hardly believe her good luck. She had actually found the secret of popularity! Like a pirate counting his booty, she rubbed her hands together and started to read. The article began:

> Why do some people seem to get all the breaks, and others struggle just to get ahead? What's the difference between the golden guy or girl, and the rest of the flock? In other words, why are some people oh-so-cool while others are just so-so? The answer is, popularity.

Eleanor nodded. Wasn't that the truth? As a so-so, she knew this firsthand. At least—she used to be a so-so. Nowadays, she wasn't sure if she rated even that.

Moving across town had killed her. Last year in the sixth grade, a lot of kids had written in her yearbook, "To a cute and funny girl." She would have been happier if they had written, "To a gorgeous babe," or "To an awesome comedian," but she could settle for "cute and funny."

If people wrote in her yearbook now, though, she

didn't know what they'd put. She could hardly get anyone at Sagamore to talk to her. Sure, kids would repeat homework assignments if she asked for them, or they would talk to her when forced to during small-group assignments in class, but what they really thought about her, she had no idea. What did they make of that disturbing light-brown mole on her upper lip? Her old best friend, Susan, had generously called it a beauty mark, but what if the new kids called it a wart?

Did the new kids think she was too short? Too pale? Too fat? A chilling thought raised goosebumps up and down her arms. Maybe the new kids had found something wrong with her that she hadn't even *thought of.* What could be worse than to be gross, and not even know it? Her stomach rolled in fear. Had she gone around acting like she was okay, when really—

Something plunked in the middle of her magazine. Eleanor jumped off the root. *Chicken*, she scolded herself, seeing it was just an acorn. Jaws clenched, she returned to the article.

> How does a person go from so-so to oh-so-cool?
> It's easy, really. All it takes is persistence and a little imagination.

Eleanor twirled her butter-colored ponytail around her fingers. Persistence. Well, that she had. Last year she had called Billy Roman every night for two weeks solid until he had broken down and agreed to "go" with her.

She liked the hand-beaded necklace he gave her that he made himself. She liked writing his name on her notebook, and seeing her name on his. She especially liked telling everyone that she had a boyfriend. But when it came right down to it, pestering Billy to go with her had turned out to be a whole lot more exciting than actually going with him. The romance lasted less than a week.

Eleanor threw an acorn toward the pond. The acorn missed, landing in some cattails. So she wasn't a romantic. But the article called for persistence, she reminded herself, not romance. She had plenty of persistence. She had plenty of that other thing she was supposed to have—imagination—too.

Eleanor was always imagining she was a pioneer girl. During her five weeks at Sagamore, she had already endured several life-threatening snowstorms, a buffalo stampede, and an Indian raid, all on her three-block walk to school. Of course, she couldn't *tell* anyone about her pretend life as a pioneer. They'd probably think she was crazy. That was the last thing she needed.

But having an imagination could be good. Her imagination had given her the idea of blowing up a dozen purple balloons and sticking them all over her purple leotard for her Halloween costume last year. After she painted her face green, even her little sister, Audrey, could figure out that she was supposed to be grapes. The balloons had helped keep her warm, too. She had been perfectly cozy running with her friends from house to house, kicking through piles of leaves, her balloons going *scrooncha-scrooncha-scrooncha*. Then Wesley Tibbs took after her with a pin. She didn't forgive him for days.

Eleanor sighed. Halloween was only one short month away, and she had no one to go trick-or-treating with. Being at home alone on Halloween—or worse, making the rounds all by herself—had to be the saddest thing in the world. She'd even wear balloons and *give* Wesley Tibbs a pin, just to have someone to go with her. But now Wesley was clear across Atlanta in Marietta. Her new house was near Decatur. Saddened, Eleanor turned back to the article.

> Imagination is important because you must draw on it to recognize what characteristics are uniquely yours. In other words, what is it about you that has the potential to attract people to you? One person may have a marvelous sense of humor. Another person's wit may prove to be irresistible. Still another person may have the all-important ability to listen to others . . .

Eleanor broke off reading, twirling her ponytail in thought. *Sense of humor, sense of humor.* Well, her Pig Face was pretty funny. She checked to see if she could still do it right.

First, accidentally pulling out a couple of eyelashes, she flipped her upper eyelids inside out. Next, she pulled up the corners of her mouth with her thumbs. Carefully—keeping the upper eyelids flipped inside out is tricky, not to mention hard on the lids—carefully, she pulled down her lower eyelids with her index fingers. Finally, she spread open her nostrils with her pinkies. With every facial feature properly pulled out of shape, she tilted her head from side to side and smiled gruesomely. Now *that* was humor.

Eleanor let go of the Pig Face and thought about other unique characteristics she had. The article mentioned wit. Chalk up another one. Why, the notes she wrote to her friends on ten-foot sections of toilet paper were absolute gut-busters. If the funny drawings in them of teachers and stuff weren't wit, she didn't know what was.

Eleanor smiled, remembering how she used to make kids laugh. Maybe, as her classmates had written in her yearbook last year, she *was* cute and funny. Maybe the kids at Sagamore just didn't know it yet.

Eleanor skipped the boring stuff about the importance of listening to others and went on reading.

> If you have trouble determining what your natural abilities might be, find a role model. Who is that golden guy or girl you so admire?

Eleanor snorted. That was easy—Misty Rice. Everyone at Sagamore admired Misty Rice. Except Eleanor was inclined to call Misty more of a silver girl than a golden girl. Misty Rice's long, perfectly straight hair was so white-blond that it shimmered like silver satin when she walked. Misty's laugh was silvery, too. It actually tinkled, like little bells. Eleanor had tried laughing like that, but she always ended up snorting. At least Eleanor's laugh wasn't as bad as Jessica's. Jessica, Misty's best friend, had a laugh that went *a-hilk a-hilk a-hilk*. The article continued:

> Once you have determined who your role model is, follow that person. Learn their secrets of success. Determine what their finest attributes are, and then study how they have used these attributes to become successful at the popularity game. More important, *make this person your friend.*

Eleanor tossed up the magazine in disgust. How? If she knew how to make Misty Rice her friend, she wouldn't have needed the article in the first place! Because, while Misty seemed as nice as she looked, there was one big problem: Jessica. Jessica guarded Misty like a bulldog.

Eleanor gathered up the magazine and flipped back to the article. She wasn't going to blow ninety-five cents of her allowance for nothing. Besides, she was desperate. She skimmed over the advice about listening to others and came to what she decided was the real meat of the article.

> Once you determine what your finest attributes are, you must be persistent—

A stick crackled nearby. Eleanor looked up, startled.

Charlie Ormsby, a sturdy, pink-faced boy in her class at Sagamore, was standing by his bike. "Are your eyes okay?" he asked.

"What do you mean?" Eleanor leaned back against the oak tree.

"I saw you do that thing to your eyes. It looked like it hurt."

Eleanor blushed, remembering her Pig Face. "It was supposed to be funny," she muttered.

"Oh." Charlie shoved his hands in his pockets.

"What are you doing here?" Eleanor asked, not bothering to be humorous or witty. Humor and wit would only be wasted on someone like Charlie Ormsby. In the five whole weeks she had gone to Sagamore, Eleanor couldn't remember seeing Charlie smile once.

Charlie glanced up shyly, then began kicking his front bicycle tire. "I'm here because of this tree," he said. "I only came because I thought nobody would be here."

"Sorry," said Eleanor. "The tree's in my yard now." An acorn dropped from the branches and bounced off Eleanor's head. She shot Charlie a look that dared him to laugh.

Charlie didn't seem to notice. "Did you know there used to be beavers in this pond?"

Eleanor perked up, interested. "Beavers? Here? I thought they all lived up in Canada or something."

Charlie shook his head. "There are lots of beavers, all over the U.S. Georgia has gobs of them—in Atlanta, even. I used to see them in"—he cleared his throat—"*your* pond, if I sat under this tree long enough."

"What do you mean, 'used to'?"

"They're gone now. The pond got messed up when they were building these houses this summer." Charlie's toe thudded against the bike tire.

From where she sat, Eleanor could see all five of the houses on her cul-de-sac. Her house was tall, new, and trimmed in lots of brass and white woodwork. She was proud of her new house. She even had her own room now—no more sharing with Audrey. Actually, her house was the only thing about moving she liked.

"My house didn't mess up your pond," she said defensively.

Charlie shrugged. "There was a dead beaver on Tyler Drive the day after they started bulldozing around the pond."

Eleanor frowned at the road that skirted the pond at the bottom of the hill: Tyler Drive. "Oh."

"That was about a year ago. I haven't seen any beavers since."

Just then, Eleanor's mother opened the kitchen door. Something the size of a small pony came bounding down the hill. It bolted past Eleanor, only to buck and leap at Charlie's feet. It licked at the air and yelped for joy.

"You know Buford?" Eleanor asked, astonished.

Charlie scratched Eleanor's Labrador retriever around the ears. "We're old friends."

Eleanor clamped her fists on her hips. She didn't know which offended her more—her own dog's preference for a stranger, or the fact that Charlie had obviously spent a lot of time hanging around her yard.

"So why bother coming back?" Eleanor snapped, watching Buford close his eyes in pleasure as Charlie scratched him under the chin. "Why bother coming back if the beavers are all gone?"

Charlie studied her for a minute as he rubbed Buford's ears. At last, he answered, "To visit the ghost."

⟦ 2 ⟧

The Thing
in the Backyard

"A ghost?" exclaimed Eleanor. She laughed out loud. So old Charlie had a sense of humor after all.

Charlie smiled politely. "Yes."

Eleanor barked out a few more guffaws, but they sounded phony even to her. She peered at Charlie. Maybe he wasn't joking. Wonderful. She had always wanted to see a ghost, but certainly not in her own backyard. Ghosts were for haunted houses, far, far away, like in London, maybe. "You really mean a *ghost?*" she asked at last.

Charlie shrugged. "I call it a ghost because I don't know what else to call it. It's not like the ghosts you see on TV. You can sort of feel it more than see it."

"Feel it?" Eleanor shivered at the thought of touching a cold, clammy spook. If she had to have a ghost in her backyard, she'd rather see it than feel it, any day.

11

"What I mean," said Charlie, "is that you just get this feeling that it's there. You don't actually touch it. If you feel anything different, it's the air. It feels, well, kind of *full*."

"You mean it's not cold and clammy?"

"Not a bit."

Eleanor sighed with relief.

Charlie cleared his throat. "So I guess you haven't noticed it."

"No." In her defense, Eleanor added, "This is the first time I've sat out here." She remembered the magazine still lying open in her lap. Casually, she covered the title of her article with her hand. An egghead like Charlie would never understand the importance of popularity.

Charlie parked his bike and sat down on the other side of it. "If this were my yard," he said, stealing a glance at Eleanor through the spokes, "I'd be out here every day."

Eleanor caught herself before she said, "Who's stopping you?" *She* was stopping him. Having Charlie Ormsby hanging around would ruin her campaign for popularity before it even got started. Okay, so he did seem kind of nice—interesting, too, if you liked ghosts and that kind of stuff. Still, the sooner she made it clear that her yard was off-limits to the Charlie Ormsbys of the world, the better.

"I think I can handle this ghost by myself," she said. She laughed lightly. "*If* there is a ghost."

"Oh, there's a ghost out here all right. From the Civil War. There was fighting, right here on this spot."

Eleanor cringed. Fighting? Guns, wounds, blood— here?

She stared at the hill that gently rose to her house. Dad cut the grass out here every weekend, and he never mentioned anything strange. They had picnics on the patio. Buford chased tennis balls. Audrey hung upside down on the swing set. Ben lifted weights. Nobody had ever noticed anything unusual. Charlie had to be crazy.

"Try closing your eyes," said Charlie. "You can see it better."

"Oh, right. What, should I just shut them like—"

Suddenly, the moment she closed her eyes, the air around Eleanor began to quiver. Like a plucked guitar string, it hummed and blurred, hummed and blurred, thickening as it vibrated. Air molecules piled on air molecules. They pressed against Eleanor's skin, weighing her down with their heaviness.

A pinging sound buzzed overhead. In her mind's eye, a boy came crashing through some bushes. He grabbed a bugle propped against a slender tree. He began blowing the horn, over and over, gasping between blasts. It shocked Eleanor to realize the boy was no older than Charlie.

"Run, Joseph, run!" a man's voice called. "It's an ambush!"

More pinging sounds whizzed overhead. Oak leaves

fluttered down, cut by something unseen. The boy looked confused, scared. Again, he brought the bugle to his lips.

Before he could blow another note, his arms flew out. He clutched his chest. Redness seeped through his fingers as his bugle rolled down the hill.

Eleanor's eyes flew open. The image of the boy dissolved like cotton candy in water. The air became lighter, thinner. The awful twanging stopped. The only sounds Eleanor could hear were her own rough breathing and the locusts, who were screaming overhead in the oak tree.

She glanced at Charlie.

"You felt it," he said. He was actually smiling.

"Felt what?" snapped Eleanor, annoyed. She certainly didn't feel like smiling.

"The ghost."

Tears sprang behind Eleanor's lids, unwelcome. "But I don't believe in ghosts!" She wiped at her eyes angrily. Charlie was making her look like a baby.

"Don't worry," Charlie said softly. "It's not going to hurt you. What you're seeing is in the past. It can't get you."

Eleanor dabbed at her nose with her knuckle. "Did you see them, too, just now?"

Charlie nodded.

"Well, what is it?" she exclaimed. "Why did the air feel so awful?"

Charlie sighed as if having to explain why the moon is round. "Well, the best I can figure is that it's time, squished together."

"How can time get squished together?"

"I don't know," Charlie said with a shrug. "Maybe it's because time flows like water, until every now and then, for some weird reason, it gets dammed up. Maybe because in certain places, too much has happened in a single space of time, so it's jammed up for all eternity. Maybe because somewhere back in time, someone's trying to reach through to the present, and that squishes time together. I don't know."

"Which do you believe?"

"All of it."

Eleanor looked sadly at her magazine. Somehow, popularity had lost its luster. "And I was worried about the future," she sighed. "Now I've got to worry about the past, too."

Charlie stood up and booted the kickstand of his bike. "Cheer up. It's a privilege to be part of the past."

Eleanor hung onto Buford's collar as Charlie bumped through the weeds around the pond down to the street below. "Sure it is," she said doubtfully.

[3]

The Toilet Paper Plan

Eleanor ran into the kitchen and slammed the door. Buford licked her hands, eager to get into the game, but Eleanor wasn't playing. Finding a ghost in her yard had left her in a sour mood.

She stood in front of the open refrigerator, letting the cool air develop her thoughts. She hadn't actually seen a ghost, she realized, at least not your typical white-sheeted moan-and-groaner. And as real as the terrible noises had seemed, she hadn't really heard anything, either. She cheered up. Maybe she'd been imagining things. She imagined things all the time.

No, that didn't help. She wilted like the head of lettuce on the third shelf of the refrigerator. Imagining that she had seen the ghost was no good. There wasn't much difference between imagining things and being crazy, and being crazy was terrible. Crazy people never get popular.

Later, as Eleanor toyed with her spaghetti at dinner, she considered taking her family out under the oak tree. If they saw the ghost, maybe she wouldn't feel so crazy. If they didn't see the ghost, well, she had better pack it up at Sagamore.

Eleanor looked at Audrey. Audrey was sipping her spaghetti until it flapped, window shade–like, at her lips. A pool of orange widened at the corners of her mouth. Eleanor snorted. Who cared if Audrey actually *was* crazy?—she *looked* crazy already.

Eleanor turned to Ben. Ben was pitching into his mound of spaghetti like a farmer pitching into a haystack. Their eyes met over his pile of pasta. "What's the matter?" he said, raising his mouth from plate level. "Can't eat your worms?" He grinned knowingly.

Eleanor scowled at her milk. She had made the mistake, once, of telling Ben that whenever she ate spaghetti, she pretended she was a bird eating worms. A spaghetti supper hadn't passed since without some kind of worm comment. If he gives you a hard time about spaghetti, Eleanor reminded herself, just think what he could do with ghosts. She wouldn't make the same mistake twice.

The phone rang.

"No calls at dinner," said Eleanor's father. He drained his glass of iced tea, unconcerned, as the phone bleated.

17

Across the table, Ben double-timed it on the pasta. He sucked in the remaining half of his pile like a vacuum. "Done!" he exclaimed, pushing away from the table. He ran for the phone.

The call was for him, as usual. The move across town hadn't killed everyone.

"I'm going back to work," said Eleanor's dad, wiping his beard with his napkin as he rose. "Dominique hasn't gotten down how to make those sausage rolls yet." Last year, Eleanor's dad had opened a restaurant called the Pizza Station. That was why they had moved—to be close to her father's work. The restaurant used to be a gas station, but Mr. and Mrs. Cotton had added red-checked curtains and tablecloths and turned it into a pizzeria. Nowadays, Dad was never around long enough to talk about normal things, let alone crazy stuff like ghosts.

Mom pushed back her empty plate and rested her elbows on the table as Mr. Cotton banged out the kitchen door. "Eleanor, who was that nice boy I saw you with out in the yard?" She smiled at Eleanor expectantly.

"No one," snapped Eleanor. There was one thing worse than worrying about her rotten social life at Sagamore: having her mother worry about her rotten social life at Sagamore. "He's nobody."

"I know him," piped up Audrey. "That's Charlie. He's a patrol on the front hall. He lets me wear his patrol belt."

Eleanor narrowed her eyes. She *would* move to a

neighborhood where kids went to the same school from kindergarten through seventh grade. She was stuck with Audrey the whole rest of the year.

"Charlie's nice," Audrey added.

"May I be excused?" Eleanor said crossly. She had been crazy to think that she could talk to her family about the ghost in the yard. She would have to suffer it out alone, the way she did all the other crises in her life.

Then, later, as she was trudging upstairs to bed, she had the worst thought of all. It froze her on the third step from the top: If the fighting Charlie had been talking about had taken place in her backyard, then it had probably taken place under her bedroom as well. Ghosts could be anywhere. Ghosts could be *everywhere*.

As long as you didn't know what had happened before, you could ignore it. But once you started thinking of what might have been, a whole flood of ghosts could come pouring in. It was like a curse.

What if a pioneer had shot a bear where her dresser stood today? What if Indians had danced around a crackling fire in the vicinity of her bean bag chair? What if a cavewoman clubbed a caveman right under her closet? The awful possibilities were endless. And now that her mind was open to the past, Eleanor feared she could never shut it.

She stood glued to her doorway. She couldn't go into her room alone. If only she was still sharing a room with Audrey!

Eleanor did the only thing she could do. She called Buford.

There was a jingling downstairs, then a click of nails on the wooden stairs. Buford appeared, head down, tail wagging.

Though Buford smelled strongly of dog, he was as good a bodyguard as she was going to get. "Good boy," she said, patting him so that he wouldn't go back to his rug in the family room. "Nice boy." She squinted at her bed.

She had never trusted that dark space between her bed and the floor, not even in her old house. It was just the right size and dark enough for something creepy. Now that she had ghosts on her brain, the space underneath her bed was doubly creepy. Who knew what might be grabbing for her ankles?

Eleanor ran for the bed at top speed. A body's length away, she twisted in the air like a pole vaulter and cannonballed right onto the middle of her bedspread. Not even the fastest ghost could have grabbed her ankle in the time it took her to hit the sheets and wrap up like a cocoon. No way was she bothering with pj's tonight.

Eleanor felt something nudge her leg through her covers. Her heart froze. *Ghosts.* Just as she drew breath to scream, the lights snapped on.

"Eleanor?" Her mother sounded surprised. "Eleanor?

I'm sorry. I didn't know you had gone to bed already. Buford, stop pestering her."

The nudging stopped. There was a thud of bones and dog tags as Buford lay down. Eleanor peeked one eye out of the covers.

"What about this magazine you just had to have at Kroger's? I found it downstairs on the couch." Mom sat on Eleanor's bed and started leafing through the magazine. She snorted. "Where do they get this stuff?"

Eleanor pulled back the sheet to her nose. She had forgotten about the magazine.

"Which article was it that you were so interested in, anyhow? Not the one about the three-year-old giving birth, I hope. Honey, you don't have to worry about a three-year-old having a baby. No one can have a baby, not until they're ready to have periods. You know that, don't you?"

Eleanor groaned inside. She had had sex education at school since fourth grade. A nurse had come to speak to them about it twice in Girl Scouts. She had had sex education so many times that she was no longer embarrassed by it, just bored.

Mom chuckled to herself. "When I was in third grade, I thought if you kissed a boy, you could get pregnant. Then I remembered that I had kissed Mike Brooks in kindergarten. Boy, was I scared. I thought sure that kiss was going to catch up with me."

21

Eleanor clicked her tongue. "Mom, I'm not an ignora-mus, you know." Eleanor had had her own pregnancy scare in the second grade—something about drinking at the water fountain after a boy—but she wasn't especially anxious for her mother to know about it.

"You're right. You're not. Good night, sweetie." Mom kissed Eleanor on the forehead. She pulled back in surprise. "Why, Eleanor, you've still got on your sweatshirt."

Eleanor faked a yawn. "I'm tired, Mom."

"Okay," said Mom, shrugging. She switched off the light and left.

Eleanor's hand sidled to the magazine which Mom had left behind. Somehow, hearing about how dumb her mom had been when she was young made her feel better. She was brave enough, now, to risk reaching out to turn on the bedside light.

> Once you determine what your finest attributes are, you must persist in making these characteristics known. If you're a great cook, for example, have guests over for dinner. If the first dinner doesn't result in invitations, have a second dinner, or a third. *Don't* give up. *Do* be creative. The road to popularity is often paved with many obstacles.

Obstacles! Eleanor snorted. Her road had boulders! She lay thinking, careful not to let any part of her body hang over the edge of the bed. She definitely couldn't cook. She had even burned Jell-O, once, in the microwave. Having dinners was out. She would have to rely upon those tried-and-true qualities for which she had become famous at her old school, her humor and wit. It was then that The Plan was born.

The urge to carry out The Plan was so strong that Eleanor was willing to brave the space under her bed. She leapt onto the floor and boldly trotted to the bathroom. She came back carrying a new roll of toilet paper like a trophy. Many sleepless but creative hours later, The Plan was ready for action.

*

It was the slowest walk to a lunchroom ever. She was stuck behind what had to be half of the boys' soccer team, and it was no use going around them. If she went around them, they might see her. If they saw her, they might laugh at her. If they laughed at her, she would die.

Eleanor hung back, her palms sweating into the eight scrolls of toilet paper that were the heart of The Plan. She tried to pretend that the sound of her jeans rubbing together was the swish of calico skirts, but failed. Walking to the General Store, a game that often amused her on her solitary travels to the cafeteria in the past, was useless at a time like this. All of her life boiled down to one single act: carrying out The Plan.

Finally, the boys from the soccer team settled themselves noisily into their seats. Eleanor made her way nervously to Misty Rice's table. She stood behind Misty, staring at Misty's earrings as she gathered her courage. Misty's earrings were shaped like begging Scotty dogs. They were as long as Eleanor's middle finger. Misty always wore fabulous earrings.

Eleanor cleared her throat. "Uh, Misty?"

Misty turned around, her Scotty dogs swinging against her neck. "Oh! Eleanor! Hi!"

Eleanor's heart swelled. Misty actually seemed happy to see her! But Misty was always nice. She smiled at Eleanor even if Eleanor was saying something stupid or doing something dumb. Once, when Eleanor had tripped over her shoestring on the way to the pencil sharpener and almost fell in front of the entire class, Misty hadn't even laughed. Eleanor had actually swum in midair, stroking like an Olympic swimmer, and Misty had just smiled.

"This is for you." Eleanor held out one of the rolled-up notes. It was wet in the middle where she had clutched it in her hand, and the word *Misty*, which Eleanor had so carefully felt-penned in red on the outside the night before, had bled. Eleanor hoped Misty wouldn't notice.

Misty delicately took the note between her thumb and forefinger.

Jessica winged her elbow into Misty's ribs. Jessica's eyes, their natural bugginess magnified by her new contact lenses, bugged even further. " Eeeuuw! What'd Mrs. Roosevelt give you? It's wet!"

"I've got one for you," Eleanor said quickly, ignoring the "Roosevelt" remark. It wasn't the first time Jessica had made fun of her name. She handed a toilet-paper roll to Jessica. That had been part of The Plan, too. *If you can't beat them, join them.*

Jessica dangled her note from her fingertips, letting it unroll. "What'd you do, Roosevelt," she said, wrinkling her nose, "use it first?"

Eleanor smiled nervously. She couldn't let Jessica's comments stop her. The final part of The Plan was yet to be completed: Make friends with *all* the girls at Misty's table. She began delivering the rest of the scrolls.

Katherine, a tall thin girl with a serious set of orthodontic headgear, pointed to the smeared brown felt pen in which her own note was addressed. "Look! I think she went number two on mine!"

The other girls screamed with laughter. Amanda, plump and red-haired, dropped her note on the table and started shooing it away as if it were a rat. Beth Ann, the one with freckles and white eyelashes, flung her note backward over her head.

Lexy stuffed hers into her milk carton, using two straws as tweezers. Meredith poked hers under her uneaten pile of Tuna Surprise.

Eleanor blinked in horror. "I didn't *use* them!" she

cried. "Not like you think! They just got a little wet in my hand, that's all!"

Jessica shrieked, "You mean, that's *sweat?* Eeeuuuw!" She wiped her hands on her jeans and gave such a fierce imitation shiver that her growing-out-permed hair shook.

Tears stung Eleanor's eyes. "They were supposed to be funny. At my old school, everyone thought they were hilarious. There's funny pictures and stuff about teachers in them." She looked at Misty for support, but Misty had turned around and was talking to Nick, a boy at the next table.

"Well, around here, we've got plenty of regular paper," growled Jessica. "We don't have to raid *the john.*"

Misty's group howled as Eleanor fled. Out of the corner of her eye she noticed that one girl at the far end of Misty's table, Rachel, had quietly tucked her toilet paper note under her black beret. She's probably saving it to laugh at me later, Eleanor thought, swallowing the huge lump in her throat.

She slunk into a seat at the table farthest away from Misty's friends. There was no one at that table except Michael Pirkle, who everyone accused of eating erasers. She didn't bother to buy a lunch. Instead, she just sat there, staring through tears at the Friends Around The World mural done by the fifth grade art classes.

⟦ 4 ⟧

The Thing Worse Than
Sitting with Michael Pirkle

Charlie slid into the seat across from Eleanor. "I liked the note." He held up the toilet paper note that had been addressed to Beth Ann.

Eleanor grabbed for it. "That's not for you! How'd you get it?"

Charlie held the length of toilet paper out of her reach. "Manna from heaven. It landed on my lunch. I almost ate it. I'm glad I didn't, though—it was funny. Can I keep it?"

Eleanor raised an eyebrow and then settled back into a lump. "Oh, I don't care."

No wonder the toilet paper notes were a flop. Charlie Egghead thought they were funny!

"Did you go back under that tree in your yard?"

Eleanor gave Charlie the evil eye. Of course she

hadn't been under that tree. She intended never to go back under that tree for the rest of her life. "No."

"Too bad. You have all that history, right in your own backyard. Don't you care?"

"No." Out of the side of her eye, Eleanor noticed that Michael Pirkle was staring at her. She stared back. Michael Pirkle dug into his Tuna Surprise.

"You do realize that Union troops marched right over your property, don't you?"

Eleanor glanced furtively at Misty's gang. They were laughing harder than ever—at her, Eleanor knew. In the midst of them Misty sat stroking her hair—an angel. *She* wasn't laughing.

"I figure the troops must have—"

"What are you, Ormsby," Eleanor cried, suddenly furious, "a junior Mr. Mandock?"

Charlie blushed, his pink cheeks turning even pinker. Mr. Mandock, a tall man with stringy black hair and a permanent frown, was their social studies teacher. Mr. Mandock claimed that he "lived and breathed for history," which seemed to Eleanor like a smelly proposition. Mr. Mandock had breath that could be smelled from two rows over.

"No," said Charlie in a wounded tone, "it's just that I enjoy—"

"If you aren't Mandock, then shut up. Can't you see that everyone hates me?" She glanced again at Misty.

Charlie turned around. Misty's gang was huddled together, talking excitedly. Jessica's loud *a-hilk a-hilk a-hilk* rang across the cafeteria. He swung back around. "Oh, don't worry about *them*. They don't like anybody. Only themselves."

"Not Misty! Misty's really nice."

Charlie turned around for a second look. He shook his head. "'Birds of a feather . . .'"

Eleanor rolled her eyes. Of course Charlie wouldn't understand. All he cared about was weird stuff like wars and history.

As if to confirm this, Charlie said, "If you don't believe me about soldiers in your backyard, read that Civil War marker up by the Gas Town gas station. It says that the Twenty-third Corps under General Thomas Schofield marched right down Briarcliff Road, right past—"

Eleanor stuck out her bottom lip and blew so hard that her bangs danced. "Don't you see that I don't care? You can take your rotten old war and stuff it!"

Charlie blinked, hurt. "I didn't know you felt that way about it." He picked up his crumpled paper bag and strode away.

"Hey, wait!" Eleanor called after him, suddenly sorry. "I didn't mean it. So where were the soldiers going? Was there a battle?"

But it was too late. Charlie dumped his crumpled bag in a trash barrel and kept walking.

Eleanor slumped in her seat. Several spaces down the table, Michael Pirkle wiped his milk mustache off with the back of his hand and stood up. As he rose, his milk carton fell off his tray and bounced off the back of a girl at the table behind him.

"Watch it, idiot!" cried the girl, flicking droplets of milk off her red sweater.

"He's a real basket case," sniffed the girl next to her.

Head down, Michael Pirkle shuffled to the trash barrel, leaving Eleanor behind at the otherwise empty table.

Eleanor sighed. There was one thing worse than sitting with Michael Pirkle at lunch.

Sitting with nobody at lunch.

[5]

The Pig

Eleanor stood at the mirror in the bathroom. First she flipped her eyelids back. Then, carefully, she hooked her thumbs on the sides of her mouth and placed her pinkies on her nostrils.

"Man, that is gross!" grunted Ben, standing in the doorway.

Eleanor quickly dropped her hands. "Quit spying on me!"

"What are you trying to do, give yourself permanent face damage?" Ben began doing push-ups against the door frame. "If you're done making yourself ugly, would you mind getting out of the bathroom? I've got to get ready for a date."

Eleanor barked out a laugh. "Oh, right. Are you picking up the lucky girl on *your* bike or *hers*?"

Ben scowled. That he only had a learner's permit was

31

a sore subject, and Eleanor knew it. He was counting down the days until his sixteenth birthday, when he could drive. "Dad's letting me drive until we get to Patty's," he muttered. "Then he's taking us the rest of the way to the movie. Why are you such a sourpuss?"

"*I'm* not the sourpuss—*you* are!" Eleanor scooted out of the bathroom, before Ben's half-hearted swing landed on her back.

But Ben was right. She was a sourpuss. She had slipped from cute and funny, to possible so-so, to sourpuss. Ben was new to his school, too, but he had gone out with his new friends every Friday night since school started. Meanwhile, she was stuck at home, getting sourer and sourer.

Still low after the toilet paper flop, she had tried calling her old best friend, Susan, after school. But Susan's mother said Susan wasn't home. Susan was spending the night with Lorraine. When Eleanor lived in the old neighborhood, Susan and she never hung around with Ant Brain Lorraine. In fact, calling Lorraine "Ant Brain" had been Susan's idea. Now Susan was staying overnight with Ant Brain, and Eleanor had nobody. It wasn't fair.

But Eleanor wasn't a quitter. After dinner, in her bedroom, a puzzled Buford called to her side, she had fished her magazine out from under her pillow. She read again what she thought was the most important part of the article on popularity. *"Don't* give up," it said. *"Do* be creative." That was how she happened to be doing the Pig Face when Ben so rudely interrupted her.

The Pig Face was a shoo-in. Once the kids at Sagamore saw it, she would be instantly elevated to Popular. She could hear Misty's silvery laugh, ringing in her success. She didn't care if she had to practice it all weekend. She'd get it down to an art, a science—to where she could flash the perfect Pig at a moment's notice. Anyway, she had nothing better to do.

The minute she heard the kitchen door slam, she slipped back into the bathroom. Ben and her dad had left for the movies. Now she could practice the Pig in peace.

She turned back her eyelids. She carefully hooked her thumbs in her mouth . . .

The bathroom door flew open. Audrey hopped up on the edge of the bathroom counter. Buford, who had been sleeping in the shower stall, got up to lick Audrey's bare toes.

"What're you doing?" Audrey asked, wiggling her toes for Buford.

Eleanor frowned, causing both eyelids to flip down. "Nothing."

"Then why are the outside of your eyelids all red?"

"They aren't red." Carefully, Eleanor flipped back an eyelid.

"Ee-uuwie! Your eye's all bloody!"

Eleanor flipped back the other lid. "That's not blood. That's just how the insides of eyes look."

Audrey made a gagging sound.

Eleanor pulled the rest of her face into a Pig. She waggled her head at Audrey.

"Ee-uuwie! Your face looks like it got caught in a blender!"

Eleanor let go of her Pig Face. "Thanks a lot. It's supposed to be funny."

"Really?" Audrey cocked her head.

"My old friends thought it was hilarious. None of them could do it as good as me, though Ant Brain Lorraine tried." Eleanor turned to the mirror to flip up her eyelids. "The secret is in keeping your eyelids up," she confided.

Audrey watched in open-mouthed admiration as her sister made another Pig Face. Gingerly, she tried to flip her own eyelid up.

"You've got to pull it out away from your eye," Eleanor instructed. "Don't be afraid to pull out a few lashes. They'll grow back."

"When?" asked Audrey.

Eleanor shrugged. "I don't know."

Soon both sisters were doing Pig Faces in the mirror. Still clutching their faces, and with Buford dancing at their feet, they ran into the hall, right into their mother, who was carrying an armful of folded laundry.

Mom shrieked. "What have you done to your faces?"

"The Pig," said Audrey. "Like it?"

"Don't you know you can permanently damage your eyes that way?" Mom yelled. She peered at Eleanor. "Is that why you're missing that clump of eyelashes?"

Eleanor and Audrey exchanged glances.

"Don't let me *ever* see either one of you *ever* doing that again!"

The girls ran giggling into Eleanor's room. Audrey sprawled on Eleanor's bed, laughing more than was really necessary, but Eleanor decided generously not to yell. Better Audrey's leg dangling over the edge of the bed than hers.

⟦ 6 ⟧
Crazy Person

On Monday, walking to school with Audrey, Eleanor worried about when she could use the Pig Face that day. One thing she knew, the Pig wasn't to be used lightly.

A person couldn't just walk into homeroom, for example, doing a Pig. That would look too crazy. Popular people don't go around looking crazy unless there's a good reason for it.

By the same token, a person couldn't just go up to Misty at lunchtime and flash her El Pig-o, either. As nice as Misty was, she'd think that person had flipped. There was a fine line between crazy and funny, Eleanor realized. The Pig Face must be handled delicately, intelligently.

Eleanor's pace slowed as they neared the school. Audrey ran ahead, dropping her backpack onto the wet grass of the schoolyard. She joined a group of second-graders trying to scramble up a scrawny crabapple tree by the front door.

Eleanor noted with pain that one of the second-graders was Jessica's little brother, Tyler. Audrey and he were hanging from the same crooked branch, grinning at each other like monkeys. Like Ben, Audrey never had trouble making new friends. Eleanor was the only social freak in the family.

Eleanor found it hard to concentrate on her schoolwork that morning. In social studies, Mr. Mandock had to call on her twice before she heard him. She had been staring at Misty's earrings—today, a string of four silver hearts linked together so that they dangled down to her shoulders—when Mr. Mandock's voice finally penetrated her ears.

"Miss Cotton, I'll ask you just one more time. What were the workers called on a feudal estate?"

Discreetly, Eleanor covered her nose with the palm of her hand. Was she the only person in the classroom who noticed Mr. Mandock's breath? She answered quickly, hoping Mr. Mandock would go on to another victim. "Smurfs," she said.

Instantly, she realized her mistake. She prayed that the class hadn't noticed.

The class roared.

Mr. Mandock scowled. "Very funny, Miss Cotton, but I doubt if a fourteenth-century *serf* would have ever heard of a Smurf. I would advise you to take this class seriously.

"Now," said Mr. Mandock, the class still sputtering with snickers, "who can answer the next question correctly: What was an owner of an estate called?"

Eleanor shriveled with shame. Why was it that when she wanted to be funny, she was a flop, and when she didn't want to be funny, she was hilarious? She hated Sagamore. Still, as Charlie answered Mr. Mandock's question, "A lord," a little voice in the back of her brain urged, *"Don't* give up. *Do* be creative."

She would use the Pig Face if it killed her.

Things went no better in English. Eleanor was so busy watching Misty and waiting for the perfect time to flash the Pig that she could barely concentrate. She had almost finished her spelling test before she realized she had been marking all of her answers since number 7 one space too low. Time was called before she had gotten even half of the answers recopied into the right spaces.

Sweat trickled down her chest as she waved her hand in the air. "Mrs. Leto, Mrs. Leto," she called. "I made a mistake. I need more time."

Mrs. Leto smiled. "Isn't that what criminals always say?"

Several kids laughed. Eleanor thought she recognized Misty's silvery giggle, but a quick check proved her wrong. Misty was busy chewing on her pearl ring as she doodled on a paper.

Still, Eleanor burned with shame. She realized Mrs. Leto was probably kidding, but she didn't like being compared to a criminal. Though humor was Eleanor's specialty, she didn't especially like being the butt of a joke.

At lunchtime, she was sitting at Michael Pirkle's table studying Misty and her friends, when Charlie plopped down across from her. Eleanor's mouth opened in protest. She was sure that it wasn't good for her future to be seen again with Charlie. People might get the wrong idea about her. They might think she was an egghead, too. On the other hand, what was worse—being thought of as an egghead or as a goof-off?

Charlie began taking things out of his bag—a Baggie of Chee-tos, a banana, a peanut butter sandwich—and spread them out in front of him. "I didn't know you were so funny. Smurfs!" His eyebrows raised in approval.

Charlie's praise warmed Eleanor's throat like cough medicine. For a moment, he actually seemed cute. She had an overwhelming urge to poke his Pillsbury Doughboy tummy. Maybe that would put a smile on his face. Instead, she reminded herself of her future.

She cleared her throat. "Uh, Charlie, I don't know if you should be sitting here."

Charlie looked over both shoulders. "Why?"

"Well . . . because I'm expecting someone."

"Oh. Who?"

Who? was right. Eleanor scanned the lunchroom.

Over by the door, she saw Audrey's class, lined up to go back to their room. Audrey had her back to Eleanor, doing something which was making Jessica's brother, Tyler, and a few other kids squirm with laughter. Several kids down the line, a mother stood holding a little boy's hand.

"My mom," lied Eleanor. "She should be here any minute."

"Okay." Charlie gathered his Baggie of Chee-tos and the banana to his chest. "Before I go, there's something you might be interested to know."

"What?" Eleanor shifted uncomfortably. He was taking so long. She hoped Misty wouldn't choose this moment to look her way.

"I hope you don't mind, but I was in your backyard Sunday. I looked for you and looked for you, but you never came."

Eleanor stared. What was he, crazy? Didn't he think she had better things to do than to hunt for ghosts?

"Anyhow, I thought you should know: I think the ghost is upset."

Eleanor gulped. "It's hanging around in my backyard," she squeaked, "and now it's *upset?*" She glanced over at Misty. Thank goodness Misty hadn't seen her lose her cool. "You think it'll go after my house?" she whispered.

Charlie shook his head. "I didn't mean that kind of upset. I mean that it's—"

"*Shhhh,*" Eleanor hissed. Misty and Jessica had gotten up and were heading their way. Instantly, Eleanor put on the smile she reserved for yearbook pictures and boy-girl parties. Now if Misty would just overlook Charlie . . .

Misty walked past, too busy talking to Jessica to notice Eleanor. Eleanor might as well have been a lump of mashed potatoes. Misty bought a carton of milk at the serving counter, and she and Jessica strolled out into the hall, where Audrey and Tyler were walking back to class. Soon Eleanor heard Misty's silvery laugh come floating from the hall. Eleanor slumped in her seat. If only she could make Misty laugh like that!

Charlie narrowed his eyes. "You still worried about *them?*"

"Not them. Her."

Charlie stood up. "I hope your mom gets here soon. She'd better hurry if you're going to have lunch together." He marched over to another table.

It's better to be alone, Eleanor told herself as she stood in the line to leave the lunchroom. A lot of great people spent a lot of their time alone. Michael Jackson, Michelangelo, the Birdman of Alcatraz. . . .

She trudged down the hall for restroom break. Though she really had to go, she decided to hold it. Misty and her friends had gone into the bathroom, and Eleanor didn't want them to hear her tinkle. She stood in front of the drinking fountains, waiting.

Misty and the girls came out and took their turns at

the double fountain. Jessica was at the fountain by herself when Michael Pirkle stepped up to the lower side. Jessica shot Misty a look, then slipped her finger off the "on" button. A jet of water splashed up into Michael Pirkle's face.

"Hey!" Michael sputtered, water dripping from his nose onto his yellow sweatshirt. "Hey!"

"Basket case!" snickered Jessica.

Most of the other girls began tittering as he stumbled away, but not Misty. She was biting her lip to hold back a smile.

Suddenly, it was as clear to Eleanor as if someone had scrawled it on the painted blocks of the wall: FLASH YOUR PIG! FLASH YOUR PIG! MAKE MISTY LAUGH—NOW!

Eleanor grabbed her eyelids. She clutched her face and spread her nose. She turned, heart racing, to Misty.

But Misty was already laughing. Next to her, Jessica was waggling her head in a perfect Pig.

Jessica dropped her hands to her sides. "You copycat!"

"But—I made it up!" Eleanor was so upset that she forgot to flip down her eyelids. After a weekend of training, they were so well behaved that they didn't budge.

"You did not!" Jessica exclaimed. "I got it from my brother at lunchtime. He showed it to me in the hall."

Eleanor's mouth worked open and closed. "Well, he got it from my sister, then! I taught it to her!"

"Good lord, Eleanor!" exclaimed Mrs. Leto, who had appeared behind Jessica. "What did you do to your eyes?"

Jessica clicked her tongue. "She's crazy."

Behind Eleanor, someone whispered, "Better put your eyelids down." Eleanor whirled around. It was Rachel, the girl from Misty's group who always wore the weird black beret.

"Your eyelids," Rachel whispered again.

Eleanor groaned as she put down her lids. What must Misty think? She was a monster, a freak, a crazy! How was she ever going to get Misty's attention now?

[7]
Drilling Through
the Rock

Eleanor lay on her bed, her magazine spread open over her chest. *"Don't give up,"* Eleanor mimicked out loud. *"Do be creative."* She sent the magazine flapping across the room like a wounded bird, rousing Buford from a nap in his now-customary corner. How was she supposed to be creative when she had run out of ideas? What do you do with people that toilet paper notes and the Pig won't soften? Getting past Jessica to Misty was like drilling through the Rock of Gibraltar.

Eleanor rolled over and propped her head on her hand. She stared absentmindedly out her window. She was never going to be able to think of something else.

A sudden movement behind the big oak caught her eye. She noticed a dented bike lying nearby.

"Charlie!" She jumped up and hurried to the window.

Charlie was tiptoeing around *her* tree, the sneak. He

seemed to be placing objects in a circle around its gnarled base. And Misty thought *she* was nuts!

Eleanor squinted her eyes. What were those things he was putting around the tree? The book she was sure about, but the narrow silver thing drew a blank. There was a Baggie full of something orange. Eleanor peered closer. Chee-tos?

"Boo!"

Eleanor yelped and whirled around. Audrey grinned from the doorway.

"Don't do that!"

"Sorry." Audrey flopped on Eleanor's bed. "What are you going to be for Halloween?"

Eleanor clicked her tongue. "You came in here to bug me about Halloween? That's a month away." She turned back to watch Charlie.

"I know. I just want to have a really good outfit this year. I'm sick of going as a cat."

"Get out of my room."

"I thought you might have a good idea for me, since you thought up that cool grape suit last year."

Eleanor glanced over her shoulder. "It *was* a pretty good costume." She returned to watching Charlie. Now he was standing in front of the book, just staring at it. The boy had definitely flipped.

"So you got any good ideas?"

Eleanor shrugged. "Go as a banana. You have that yellow jogging suit."

"Got any other ideas besides fruit?"

"Stripe yourself green. Go as a cucumber."

Audrey snorted. "Tyler's birthday is on Halloween, and he's going to have this really neat party. I'm not going as fruits or vegetables."

Eleanor swung around from the window. "You say Tyler's going to have this party—Tyler Grenzig, Jessica's brother?"

"I don't know any other Tylers."

"Is Jessica going to be there?"

"I don't know. I don't think so. Who wants their rotten old sister around?"

The solution plunked Eleanor on the head like an acorn falling from the oak tree. She would have a Halloween party! What better way of getting to Misty?

"Why are you staring at me like that?" Audrey asked.

"Like what?"

"Like you've seen a ghost or something."

In her spookiest voice, Eleanor warbled, "I am a ghost!" She lifted her arms and chased Audrey out of the room and down the hall.

Eleanor kept going until she was on the patio. She slid onto the empty frame of a redwood lawn chair, covering her mouth to hush her loud breathing. There, from behind the gas grill, she could keep an eye on Charlie while she planned her party.

Charlie had now moved in front of the Baggie of

Chee-tos. Eleanor watched, fascinated, as Charlie stared at the bag. "I'm here, Joseph," he said. He shut his eyes.

Eleanor clicked her tongue. He had to be kidding. Charlie glanced up. Eleanor ducked, too late.

"Hi, Eleanor!" he called across the yard. "You don't mind me using the tree, do you?"

Mind? Of course she did. Eleanor had a party to plan, a party that might make the difference between being a basket case and being popular. If only Charlie wasn't so darn sincere. She tried to look fierce. "What are you doing?"

Charlie stepped forward. "I'm trying to see what's happened to our ghost."

Eleanor shrunk back. "Don't go calling it *our* ghost!" she warned. "It's your ghost, not mine!"

"Oh . . . well, thank you." Charlie scooped up the Baggie of Chee-tos. "I guess these aren't working. I didn't think they would."

Eleanor didn't want to encourage him, but her curiosity won out. "What wasn't working?"

"The Chee-tos. The book didn't work either. I was just about to get to the harmonica."

"I don't get it."

Charlie galloped toward her, almost stumbling in his eagerness. "I told you that I thought the ghost was upset for some reason, right? Well, the reason I think so is because each time I come here, I see less and less of him. It's been that way for months. I used to see soldiers picking blackberries, soldiers swimming, stuff like that. Now—hardly anything."

"You mean there was *more?*" Eleanor felt sick.

"Lots. Anyway, Sunday I was sitting under our— my—*your* tree, trying out my new harmonica, when all of a sudden I saw Joseph real good. Almost like old times."

"Who's Joseph?"

"The ghost."

Eleanor snorted. Charlie was getting almost dangerously nutsville. Calling a ghost by name!

"So now I'm trying the process of elimination. I had this book with me"—he held up *The Red Badge of Courage*—"and some Chee-tos, so it could have been any of the three. I usually don't bring anything, except Chee-tos, maybe, and Buford usually takes care of them before I sit down. So I'm wondering which thing Joseph may have liked: The book? The Chee-tos? The harmonica? Personally, I'm rooting for the harmonica."

Eleanor looked longingly toward her house. She could have been inside, planning her party, but no, she had to come out to spy on a madman. It never paid to be nosy.

"I'm about to try the harmonica. Would you like to come?"

"Thanks but no thanks." Eleanor got up and edged toward the house.

48

"It won't hurt you," Charlie called after her. "Come on back here and—"

Eleanor turned and ran. She slammed the door shut. Outside, she could hear the faint sound of "Taps" being blown on a harmonica.

She slumped against the door. Why couldn't her life be normal, like Misty's? Misty didn't have a ghost in her backyard. Misty didn't have some crazed boy laying offerings around her tree. Misty shopped for earrings . . . hung around with her friends . . . talked to boys—in short, did all the normal, fun things Eleanor was dying to do. And what was Eleanor stuck with? An egghead and a ghost. It wasn't fair.

Eleanor heard a flapping sound behind her. A pink flowered sheet was drifting through the kitchen. Buford pranced behind it, nipping at the hem. "Woooooooo," came a moan from under the sheet.

Eleanor clicked her tongue. "Very funny, Audrey, but somehow I don't think the flowers are going to cut it."

"I'm a designer ghost," came a wavery voice.

"Right."

Audrey flipped the sheet back from her face. "I thought you'd like it. You made me think of it when you chased me out of your room, acting like a ghost."

"Why can't everybody just shut up about ghosts?"

"I just wanted a good Halloween suit," Audrey protested.

49

Suddenly, like another acorn falling from the oak, another brilliant idea hit Eleanor. Why not have her Halloween party outside, in the yard, and get the ghost to show up *on purpose!*

Eleanor shook her head in disbelief. How had she been so dumb? She had popularity insurance, right under her nose! If she had to have a rotten old ghost, why not use him to her advantage? So what if she personally hated "Joseph"? Everyone else would love him. Everyone—except her—loved to be scared.

"Why do you look so funny?" said Audrey, wrinkling her nose.

"Ever see somebody whose dream is about to come true?"

Audrey cocked her head. "Uh-uh."

"Well," said Eleanor, grinning her best yearbook grin, "you're looking at one now."

[8]

Bob Hope

Eleanor sat on her bed, her legs folded tightly underneath her, coloring in the letters of her eighth invitation. The tip of her tongue peeked out between her lips, as it always did when she was concentrating hard. After a long session of concentration, she'd often end up with chapped lips. Her lips were a mess last year after she finished her social science project paper ("What Was Pioneer Life Like in Georgia?"). They were already starting to sting, and she still had three more invitations to go.

She allowed herself a glance out the window. When she had started on the invitations after dinner, it had been light outside. Now it was dark, very dark. Eleanor hated the dark. With darkness came things you couldn't see. She tucked her feet under her legs even tighter, and started in on the next invitation.

There were to be eleven invitations in all: eight for Misty and her friends, and three for the boys Misty and her friends took turns liking. Each invitation was carefully drawn on a folded piece of notebook paper and looked like this:

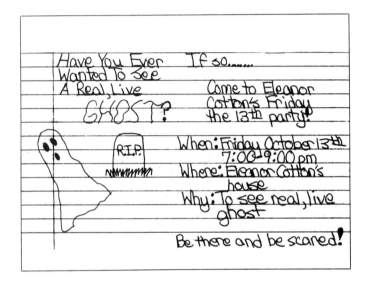

At dinner, when Eleanor had asked her parents for permission to have the party, Ben had laughed. "You're having a Halloween party on October thirteenth? I may be crazy or something, but aren't Halloween parties supposed to be on Halloween?"

"Everyone has Halloween parties on Halloween," Eleanor said indignantly. "I wanted to be different. I thought since the thirteenth was going to be on a Friday this year, that would be spooky enough."

Of course, the real reason Eleanor wanted the party on the thirteenth was because she couldn't wait all the way until Halloween to become popular. Waiting till the thirteenth would be hard enough, and the thirteenth was only ten days away.

Mom got up and looked at the wall calendar. "I don't have anything going on the thirteenth."

Dad took another bite of lasagna. "Me neither." He wiped his beard with his napkin. "I'll get Dominique to cover for me, so I can be here to help."

Eleanor smiled gratefully. Friday was the busiest night at the Pizza Station.

Mom sat back down at the table. "Okay, Eleanor, you're on. How many kids did you have in mind?"

"Oh, about eleven."

"Can I come?" Audrey asked.

"No!"

Ben got up, groaning. "I'll be sure not to be here. Eleven goofy little preteens—yuk!" He dropped his plate into the sink with a clatter.

"Good! I don't want an overgrown idiot here, either!" Eleanor had cried. But now, as she worked on the invitations in the dark of the night, she wished she had asked Ben to stay. Ben was brave.

The morning of the first day of school, when Eleanor had been in a panic about going to a new school, Ben calmly ate pancakes as if he went to new schools every day. "If anyone gives you a rough time," he told her, washing down the sixth pancake with a king-size mug of milk, "just tell them to shove it."

That's how Ben would be if the ghost showed up. "Hey, ghost," Eleanor could hear him say. "Shove it!"

*

The next day in social studies, a tired Eleanor hunched at her desk. Though her mother had ordered her to stop, she had worked on secretly, finishing her invitations by the glow of the hall light. She couldn't sleep after that. The plans for her party had whirled around and around her head, until finally a new and horrible realization knocked the party plans clear out of her mind. Having a ghost party meant having *a ghost*. Having a ghost meant that she would have to meet Joseph, again, *at night*.

Now Mr. Mandock's breath penetrated Eleanor's worries. "Miss Cotton, please tell us—who was the most important individual in the Western World during the Middle Ages?"

Eleanor stared blankly. She had heard Mr. Mandock's voice, but the words hadn't soaked in. One row over and two people back, Charlie whispered the answer.

Desperate, Eleanor repeated what she thought she heard. She cleared her throat.

"Bob Hope."

For a split second, everything was quiet. Mr. Man-

54

dock's mouth hung slightly ajar. The class held its breath.

"The pope!" Charlie whispered again, this time loud enough for Eleanor to hear. Eleanor slid down in her seat.

Mr. Mandock's mouth snapped shut. "Cotton, put your name on the board!"

Like a volcano, first the class hissed, then it erupted.

"Next person who laughs," warned Mr. Mandock, "puts his name under hers."

Eleanor was miserable, but wide awake, the rest of the morning.

As the class headed to the cafeteria at lunchtime, Eleanor slipped into line two people behind Rachel. Rachel always seemed to be at the end of Misty's pack, just on the edge of popularity. That's not where *she* was going to be when *she* was Misty's friend, Eleanor decided. She was going to be right up there, next to Misty, just like—

Jessica's laugh echoed down the hall. *A-hilk!*

Eleanor sighed. It wasn't going to be easy.

The class passed the drinking fountain. Since the Pig Face flop, the very sight of the drinking fountain caused a tiny bomb to explode in Eleanor's gut. Her grip tightened on the library book which held the invitations. She knew better now than to hold them in her sweaty hand.

The roar of the lunchroom greeted her ears. Misty's

gang strolled to their table in the center of the room and set down their lunches. They were settling into their seats when Eleanor got up enough courage to stand behind Misty.

"Look behind you," said Jessica, pointing over Misty's shoulder. "It's Bob Hope."

Eleanor blushed as Misty turned around. Misty smiled.

Jessica's eyes narrowed. "Geeze, Bob," she sneered, "I don't know if we can take any more of your weird jokes."

Eleanor felt tears gathering behind her lids. *Don't* give up. *Do* be creative. She took a deep breath and opened her book, trying her hardest to ignore the snarl on Jessica's face. "I've got some invitations for you all."

Misty took her invitation without comment. With her stomach floating in her throat, Eleanor handed out the rest.

Jessica took one look at her invitation and slapped it shut. "Bob, is this another one of your stupid jokes?"

"No," Eleanor stammered. "I'm serious."

Jessica tossed her invitation in the air. "You expect us to believe in *ghosts?*"

Eleanor swallowed. "Well, yes. I've seen—well, actually felt—it. Kind of."

"Wow," said Misty, her eyes round. "How could you stand it?"

"'I felt it,'" Jessica mimicked. "'I felt it.' Now I suppose you're going to tell us it was all cold and gooey."

Eleanor shook her head fiercely. "That's how I thought a ghost would be, too! Only it wasn't. You don't actually *feel* anything."

Jessica arched a brow. "You just said you felt it."

Eleanor stood, stunned. Before she could think of an explanation, at the other end of the table Rachel said, "I'll go."

The other girls turned to stare at Rachel in disbelief.

"You will?" said Beth Ann.

"You've got to be kidding," sniffed Jessica.

"I think it sounds neat," Rachel said, adjusting her beret over her tangly dark hair. "I always wanted to meet a ghost. They must be real sad, to be dead and all."

Jessica rolled her eyes. "I swear, Rachel. Everything's sad to you!"

"I want to go, too."

Now everyone turned to stare at Misty.

Beth Ann asked, "You do?"

"Yes," said Misty. "What else are we doing Friday the thirteenth?"

"I thought we were going roller skating!" said Jessica.

Misty shrugged. "We do that every Friday."

Eleanor smiled at Misty gratefully.

Jessica frowned. "Oh, all right. I'll go, too. But on one condition." She scowled at Eleanor. "That this isn't another one of your stupid jokes."

"It's not! I promise!" Happily, Eleanor skipped over to the empty end of Michael Pirkle's table, her regular spot.

Michael stopped grazing on his coleslaw long enough to smile. Even though bits of slaw dripped from the corners of his mouth, Eleanor smiled back. Why not? It wouldn't be long until she was out of there!

[9]

A Real Basket Case

After lunchtime, as Eleanor's class was being herded to the bathrooms, Charlie slipped behind Eleanor in line.

"Pssst—Eleanor."

Eleanor froze. This was not a good time to be seen with Charlie. In fact, no time was a good time to be seen with Charlie.

"I heard Misty say she was going to your house for a party."

Eleanor felt heat rising to her face. For some odd reason, she felt guilty for not inviting Charlie. After all, he had introduced her to the ghost. Still, no way could she risk having him come. What would Misty think if Egghead Charlie showed up?

Charlie blushed. "I wasn't trying to get you to invite me or anything," he muttered.

Eleanor kept walking. After a moment, Charlie whispered, "Misty said you were going to look for a ghost."

"What's it to you?" Eleanor whispered back, stung with guilt.

From the head of the line, Mrs. Leto warned, "Quiet in the hall!"

"I've got a good idea about how to make sure Joseph shows," Charlie whispered.

"Thanks but no thanks."

Mrs. Leto turned around. "Eleanor, quiet!"

Eleanor felt her skin pinken.

"I just want to help," Charlie whispered. "If you let me—"

"No!" Eleanor interrupted. "Now, shhhh! You're getting me in trouble!"

"If you don't do something about it, you may not see Joseph at all. I'm not sure how much longer he's going to stick around."

Eleanor whirled around. "What do you mean, he's not going to stick around? He better stick around—at least until Friday the thirteenth, he better! After that, I don't care where he goes!"

"Eleanor!" called Mrs. Leto. "That's one check mark!"

Eleanor scowled at her shoes. Great. Now she looked like a goof-off again. She was never going to make it at Sagamore!

*

Eleanor could barely drag herself down the sidewalk as she left school that day. An image of herself in a long gingham dress and bonnet, walking alongside an ox-drawn wagon, flickered in her mind, then died like a spent sparkler. Her pretend life on the prairie was over. The party consumed all her thoughts now. It was her only hope.

Audrey dropped from the schoolyard crabapple tree as Eleanor walked by. She was wearing a yellow hard hat which was so big it hung down to her nose. She tipped back her head to see. "Like my hat?" she asked.

"No," grumped Eleanor.

"Tyler brought it to show-and-tell today. It's his dad's."

"Give it back and come on, or I'm walking home without you."

Audrey trotted back to the tree and handed the hat to Tyler, who was hanging one-armed from a branch. She scooped her backpack off the grass and caught up with Eleanor.

"Tyler loves me," Audrey announced. "Everyone says."

Eleanor walked on in sullen silence.

One block from home, a dented bicycle skidded to a stop beside her. "Sorry Mrs. Leto yelled at you," Charlie said, panting.

Eleanor quickened her pace, but Audrey lagged behind. "Hi, Charlie! Can I wear your patrol belt?"

61

"Not now," said Charlie. "Eleanor, wait! It's important!"

Eleanor stopped. "You won't be happy until everyone hates me, will you?"

Charlie looked confused.

"Just leave me alone!" Eleanor stomped forward.

Charlie ran his bike beside her, trying to keep up. "I don't blame you for being mad, but I didn't get to tell you the most important part. About what I found out when I was testing stuff under the tree."

Eleanor kept on stomping.

"Eleanor, the harmonica worked! When I started playing 'Taps,' I saw more of Joseph. Well, not really *more*, I guess, but at least not *less*. Last few times, all I've seen was—"

Eleanor whirled around. "Charlie Ormsby, would you shut up? You're nuts! Absolutely nuts!"

As she marched away, an awful little voice nagged in her ear. If Charlie was nuts, she was just as nutty. After all, she'd seen Joseph, too.

Charlie didn't follow. Eleanor wasn't sure if she was relieved or disappointed. Either way, a new problem had her occupied. What if she and Charlie were the only nutty ones? What if everyone she invited came to her party, but she was the only one who saw Joseph? That would be worse than not having the party at all.

And what if not even she could see Joseph, because

he had disappeared, as Charlie warned? Once upon a time, in the good old days before she announced her party, that would have been good news. But now she was stuck. As much as she feared him, she *needed* Joseph. He just had to appear. He had to!

⟦ 10 ⟧
Pigs or Cows?

Mom stood facing Eleanor with hands on hips. "Are you sure you want your party outside? It's supposed to get pretty cold tonight. We can move everything inside, you know."

Even as she was tying the last bunch of black and orange balloons to the flagpole at the edge of the patio, Eleanor could hardly believe the day of the party had arrived. Ten sleepless nights, ten cringing days, had passed in a painful blur. Now, as she struggled with the balloons bobbing in her face, a single chant gave her courage: *Don't* give up. *Do* be creative.

"Eleanor? Do you want to move your party inside or not?"

"Keep it outside," Eleanor said quickly. "We're going to . . . play games." Somehow, Eleanor had never been able to bring herself to mention to her mother that there was a ghost in their backyard. Her mother cherished the mistaken idea that Eleanor was normal.

Mom sighed contentedly, gazing in the direction of the HAPPY FRIDAY THE 13TH banner Eleanor had strung between two dogwood saplings in the yard. "Your first boy-girl party . . ."

"Mom!" Eleanor objected. Her mother seemed happier about her party than she was. "Just keep Audrey inside, would you? Buford, too."

Mom began pulling at her chin the way she always did when she was thinking. "Let's see now—the guests are coming at seven. Dad will have hot dogs on the grill by seven-fifteen, and then everyone leaves at nine. What do you plan to do in between?"

Eleanor tamped down the awful feeling of terror that was simmering just below the surface. "Don't worry. I've got it all planned."

A few minutes later, at the bathroom mirror, Eleanor brushed her hair into a ponytail for the fifth time. She ran over the plans she had sweated out for ten nights straight. From 7:00 to 7:30, they'd dance. From 7:30 to 8:00, they'd eat. From 8:00 to 9:00, they'd ghost hunt. From 9:00 to eternity—if everything worked out right—she'd be an important member of Misty Rice's group, maybe even Misty's best friend.

The doorbell rang. A solitary bubble of fear broke

loose and settled in her throat. She stumbled down the hall, tripping over Buford, who always made it his business to be at the door first.

"What a cute dog!" Rachel exclaimed, as Eleanor opened the door. Buford's tail bashed Eleanor's leg in greeting. When Rachel bent over to pet him, Eleanor noticed Rachel had fastened a tiny white ghost pin to her beret.

"Don't tell me I'm the first one here?"

Eleanor nodded, too terrified to speak.

"Misty and Jessica and the rest should be here in a minute, then. Misty's mom's driving. I came straight from my piano lesson. I hope I'm not too early."

Eleanor looked at her watch: 6:50. "You're okay," she managed to say. "You can help me set up my brother's tape player. Stay, Buford."

Buford followed cheerfully as Eleanor led Rachel out to the patio. Eleanor set Ben's tape player on a card table and turned the volume on high. Once the music was blaring properly, she wandered over to the picnic table where Rachel was scratching Buford's ears. It occurred to Eleanor that if Charlie was right about music, maybe the ghost would like Ben's tapes. Surely, he—it—Joseph—would show tonight, even for just a second.

Rachel asked, "Is there really a ghost?"

Eleanor stiffened. It was as if Rachel had read her mind. "I saw it myself," she croaked, "a few weeks ago."

"Is it real scary?"

Eleanor's heart pounded, remembering. "Real."

"What kind of ghost is it?"

"Civil War," Eleanor gulped. She looked at her watch: 7:00.

"Cool!" breathed Rachel. "I love the Civil War. I love history." She shrugged happily. "Sometimes I just pretend that I'm living back in time."

Eleanor stared. No. She'd better not admit that she played pioneer girl. Not yet. Not to a stranger. She hadn't even told Susan about that.

"History makes me so sad," Rachel sighed. "To think of all those people, living and dying, living and dying. I mean, what do they have to show for it? Nothing. Just living and dying, living and dying. It's so *sad*."

A movement at the kitchen window caught Eleanor's eye. It was Audrey, flashing a Pig.

Eleanor narrowed her eyes threateningly, but it was too late. Rachel turned and saw Audrey. Audrey ducked, leaving the kitchen curtains swinging.

"Little sisters," Rachel sympathized. "They're such pests, you know?"

A few painfully quiet minutes passed. Then Eleanor's dad stepped out onto the patio carrying a plate stacked with hot dogs. "Who's hungry?"

"I am," Rachel said politely.

"So where's the party?" Dad asked, embarrassingly jovial. "Or are you two going to boogie alone?"

Eleanor shrugged. It was best to pretend that her father

67

was actually cool. "They're coming. They're just late." She only wished that she could believe that.

"Do you want me to put the dogs on, then?" Dad asked.

"Go ahead," said Eleanor, looking at her watch: 7:10. Best to have the food ready so that when everyone arrived, the party could stay on schedule.

"Can you believe this?" said Mr. Cotton, loading the grill with hot dogs. "A man with a pizza restaurant, serving hot dogs at his daughter's party! She wouldn't let me bring pizzas. Said it would look like we were advertising!"

Eleanor cringed, but Rachel only said, "I love pizza. Give me a Vegetarian Special any day."

At 7:50, the hot dogs looked like so many pieces of withered black leather. Dad plunked them on a plate and set them in front of Eleanor and Rachel.

"Sorry, Ellie. Couldn't keep them on the grill any longer." He exchanged glances with Mom, who was standing next to him, pulling her chin.

"I like 'em black," chirped Rachel. She put one of the hot dog remains on a bun. "Then they don't look so much like meat. I hate to think I'm eating an animal. It's so sad, don't you think?"

Eleanor stared at the strip of charcoal lying on her own bun. The sadness of eating animals was one form of sadness that hadn't occurred to her that evening. She put the hot dog back down on her plate.

Rachel eyed Eleanor as she bit into her hot dog.

"Don't worry, they'll be here," she said with her mouth full. "Sometimes Misty forgets what time it is. She's late all the time. No big deal."

Mom cleared her throat. "No. It is a big deal. When an invitation says seven, a person should be there at seven. It's common courtesy."

"Mom!" Eleanor protested under her breath, horrified.

"Dinner parties especially," Mom continued. "You should never come late to a dinner party."

Between clenched teeth, Eleanor said, "Mom, this isn't a dinner party."

Mom shook her head. "If you're serving food, it's a dinner party. I'd say some of your new friends are pretty rude."

Eleanor felt her face turning the color of a properly cooked hot dog. If her mom thought that she was making her little baby feel better by cutting down Misty, she was dead wrong.

"You're right, Mrs. Cotton," Rachel agreed. "People should come on time to dinners. It's so sad when people hurt other people by not thinking."

"Who's hurt?" said Eleanor, jumping up. She ran over to change the tape, which had now played in its entirety at least twice. Her hands shook as she tried to jam the new tape into the player. She looked at her watch: 7:57.

Eleanor sat down at the table and watched as Rachel calmly ate two more hot dogs. "What do you think these dogs used to be?" Rachel asked between bites. "Pigs or cows?"

At 8:10, Eleanor heard car doors slam out front. Mom, who'd evidently been listening too, sprinted inside. Soon there was laughter in the house, coming closer. Eleanor held her breath. Her entire future depended on the next few minutes.

[11]

The Thing in the Bushes

Eleanor's mother looked as nervous as Eleanor herself as she struggled to pull Buford back into the house. The patio door slammed behind Misty and her friends.

"Hey, Bob Hope!" said Jessica. "How's it going?"

Nick stood behind Misty in a pack with the two other boys. He snickered into his hand. "Bob Hope!" As if on cue, Theo and Grant chortled.

Jessica beamed. "I used to call her 'Mrs. Roosevelt.' Get it?"

"You're late, you guys," said Rachel, not smiling. "And she was serving dinner, too."

Misty grimaced. "Sorry!"

Even in her embarrassment, Eleanor noticed Misty's earrings. They were shaped like four-inch wind chimes.

"So where's the ghost?" asked Jessica, looking around.

"Yeah, we want to see the ghost!" said Nick.

"WoooOooOooooo!" he warbled, making the other new arrivals laugh.

"Not here," Eleanor managed to stammer. She pointed toward the oak tree. "Out there."

"All right!" said Nick, slapping Theo's hand. "Let's get him!" He ran for the tree. "WoooOooOooooo!"

Soon almost everyone was warbling. They ran for the tree like hounds on a hunt. "WoooOooOooooo!" Eleanor followed, her stomach bubbling with fear.

They stood under the oak tree, panting. Above them, the branches groaned in the breeze, invisible in the dark. Nick made a little whistling noise through the space in his front teeth. "Well," he said, "I don't know about you, but I don't see nothing."

"Shut up, Nick," said Jessica. "How can I hear Bob Hope's dumb old ghost when you're talking?"

Theo snorted. "You shut up, Jessica. How can I hear Bob Hope's dumb old ghost when *you're* talking?" He glanced at Nick for approval, but Nick only whistled through his teeth and gazed up into the branches.

"Excuse me." Eleanor cleared her throat. "Excuse me, but if you want to see the ghost, you'd better close your eyes."

Jessica clicked her tongue. "Close our eyes? Hope, is this some kind of trick?"

"No," Eleanor stammered. "Remember?—I told you. It's not the kind of ghost like they have on TV. You have to kind of imagine him, like in your head."

"Imagine him?" Jessica exclaimed. "Imagine him? You mean we came all the way over here to *imagine* a ghost? How tacky! We thought we were going to see a real, live ghost!"

"Shhh!" said Rachel. "I can't concentrate."

"He's real!" whispered Eleanor, her voice failing her. "I've seen him. Just not with my eyes."

Theo flicked back the black bangs that hung in a curtain over his eyes. "This is stupid."

"A stupid girl party," said Grant.

"Who you calling stupid?" said Beth Ann. "Boys are stupid. Girls are smart."

Nick shrugged, making his Braves jacket rustle. "If you're so smart, what'd you get on your last science test?"

"An eighty-five."

"*I* got an eighty-seven. What'd I tell you—boys are smarter!"

"Wait a minute," said Katherine. "I got a ninety-two."

"So, I got a ninety-two, too," said Theo. They stared at each other as if getting identical grades was a sign from heaven.

"Tough," said Jessica. "Rachel got a hundred. Didn't you, Rachel?"

Rachel didn't answer. She was leaning against the tree with her eyes closed.

Misty sniffed. "I think we should listen for the ghost. That is what we came here for, isn't it?"

The others shifted uncomfortably.

73

"Well, okay then. Let's shut our eyes." Misty closed her eyes. Eleanor couldn't help but notice how prettily Misty's lashes swept against her cheek.

"Brother!" Jessica muttered. She eased her eyes into a begrudging squint.

Eleanor took a deep breath. She shut her eyes.

Suddenly, there was a thickening in the air. The very molecules seemed to hum. The air became heavy, heavier. . . .

First Eleanor heard a pinging sound, then she saw the boy. He stood under the young tree, wild-eyed, gasping for breath. He brought his bugle to his lips—

A hand clutched Eleanor's arm. Eleanor's eyes flew open. The boy dissolved.

Misty tugged at Eleanor's arm. "Eleanor, listen! Do you hear something?"

It took Eleanor a moment to calm down enough to separate past from present. Then, over the thumping of her pulse in her ears, she heard it. A soft strain of music wafted through the breeze.

"I know that tune!" Nick whispered.

"Me, too," said Grant. "Boy Scout camp—they played it before we went to bed."

"'Taps,'" hissed Theo.

Misty whispered to Eleanor, "Does your ghost play 'Taps'?"

Eleanor bit her lip. The music did sound familiar. . . .

"Look!" Jessica whispered. "In those bushes over there. Something's moving!"

Misty and Jessica hugged each other tight. Beth Ann put her hands over her eyes. Katherine started crying. Lexy, Meredith, and Amanda held hands. The boys edged together in a tight little knot.

"It *is* moving!" whispered Theo.

Nick gasped, "The ghost!" He looked at Misty and then straightened his Braves jacket. "Well, I'm not afraid!" he said in what would have been a manly voice had it not squeaked at the end. He snatched up a stick. "Come on out, ya ghost! Come on out and see what ya get!"

A white shape hovered behind the bushes. Eleanor held her breath.

"Come on out now!" said Nick, voice quavering. "I'm not going to hurt you!"

The whiteness in the bushes seemed to quiver.

"Come on, ghooooo—"

Just then, the kitchen door opened. "No, Buford!" Eleanor's mother cried. A black streak sped for the bushes. It leaped upon the white thing, knocking it down. The white thing struggled up. It staggered toward Nick.

"Noooooo!" Nick yelled, holding his hands in front of his face. "Noooooo! Stay away!"

The white thing lurched forward. Nick screamed and

scrambled backward. He tumbled flat on his back. The rest of the gang—except for Rachel—started running.

"Wait, everybody!" the thing in white called, fending off Buford with his arm. "Hey, wait! It's me!"

Nick rose up on this elbow. "Charlie?"

Charlie stuffed his harmonica into the pocket of his white nylon jacket with one hand, and held Buford down with the other. "I didn't mean to scare anybody. I only came to help Eleanor."

Over on the patio, Jessica strained her neck forward to see. "Eleanor Cotton!" she shouted after a second. "What a cheap trick! Planting Charlie in the bushes!"

Some of the girls giggled nervously.

"It's not funny!" Jessica snapped.

"Jessica, no! You think—? You thought—?" Charlie slapped his hand to his cheek. "Eleanor didn't know about me—honest! It was my idea to come here and play my harmonica. The ghost likes 'Taps.' I thought it would help you all to see him. He's not been showing himself like he used to."

"'Not been showing himself,'" Jessica mimicked. "Humph! How stupid do you think we are? There's no ghost! There never will be! Come on everybody, I'm going!" Jessica flounced toward the gate.

Misty looked apologetic. "Sorry, Eleanor, but I didn't see him either. Are you *sure* there's a ghost? I mean, maybe you just *thought* you saw a ghost. People *think* they see ghosts all the time."

Eleanor wiped away tears with the back of her hand. She couldn't speak. A hard, salty lump had taken her throat prisoner.

"But there *is* a ghost!" exclaimed Charlie. "From the Civil War! His name is Joseph."

"Joseph?" Misty laughed her silvery laugh. "Oh, Charlie!"

A knowing grin slowly spread across Nick's face. "Charlie lo-oves El-ea-nor! Charlie lo-oves El-ea-nor!"

Charlie's face almost glowed in the dark. "Stop it!" he yelled, chasing Nick out the back gate. "Shut your mouth!"

The other boys followed, singing, "Charlie lo-oves El-ea-nor!"

"He does not!" Eleanor cried, watching Misty and her friends drift toward the gate.

"Hurry up, Rachel! Misty's leaving!" Beth Ann called toward the tree where Rachel was still standing.

Like a robot, Rachel walked back to the patio. Her eyes were as round as acorn tops. She had taken off her beret and was wringing it in her hands. Eleanor noticed that the beret was shaking.

"You all go ahead," Rachel called in a quivery voice. "I'll get my mom to come get me."

"Good, 'cause we're leaving," said Jessica. "Hope, you got a phone?"

⟦ 12 ⟧
July 19, 1864

Charlie kicked at the wheel of the portable grill on the patio. With each kick, bits of dried and blackened hot dog flaked from the bars of the grill down into the ashes below. "I said I was sorry," he said. "I thought I would be helping. I never thought they'd actually see me."

Eleanor hunched on the redwood lounge chair nearby. She gave Charlie a sharp look out of the corner of her eye and then went back to watching the hot dog bits flaking into the grill.

In a redwood rocker across from Eleanor, Rachel sat biting her nails. Rachel was the only reason Eleanor was not up in bed, crying her eyes out. Until Rachel's mom came, Eleanor had to keep up appearances. She didn't know why Rachel hadn't left with the others. She should be off with the rest of Misty's group, laughing and making fun of Eleanor like the rest of them. Except for Misty. Misty was always nice.

"It's just that I was afraid the ghost wouldn't come," Charlie said. "It's not as regular as it used to be, that's the problem. I thought if I played 'Taps,' then everyone might be able to see it. I know how much having everyone see it meant to you."

Eleanor snorted. Only her life.

"Excuse me," said Rachel, but there's something you two should know."

Eleanor and Charlie turned.

"I saw something out there."

Charlie stopped kicking the grill. "You did?"

"You did?" Eleanor echoed.

"Uh-huh. I just didn't want to say anything in front of Jessica."

An ally! Yes! Eleanor had to stop herself from raising her arms in victory.

"Well, actually, I felt it more than saw it, you know what I mean?"

Eleanor grinned. "Oh, yes. I know exactly what you mean."

Charlie's toe jiggled against the grill. "Uh, Rachel, just exactly what did you see?"

"It was so sad!" Rachel twirled her hair around her fingers. "I heard this kind of pingy sound, you know? But before I could figure it out, this guy came crashing through the bushes. He wasn't very old, you know—kind of cute, too. He seemed real hot on getting this bugle that was propped against a tree."

Rachel shuddered. "Then it got real gross. He grabbed his chest, and this blood came oozing out between his fingers. Yuk! The next thing I knew, Nick was lying on the ground in front of me. I thought someone had shot him, too."

Charlie nodded. "That's what I was afraid of."

"Oh, Nick wasn't shot!" Rachel exclaimed.

"That's not what I meant," said Charlie. "What I meant was, I was afraid that was all you saw. Eleanor, when you saw the soldier the other day, how much did you see of him?"

"His whole body." She shrugged. Now, if she could just get Rachel to tell Misty—

"No, I mean what was he doing when you first saw him?"

"Same as Rachel." Eleanor smiled at Rachel apologetically. If Charlie didn't shut up soon Rachel would think they were both nuts.

Charlie nodded. "Just what I thought. Do you know that before they started building Eleanor's house last summer, I used to be able to sit under that tree and see everything? You know how it would start? Joseph was picking blackberries. He just wandered up and started picking blackberries."

"Poor guy," Rachel murmured.

Eleanor's eyes widened. Rachel was buying it!

"He was a real boy, Rachel," Charlie said. "Back on July 19, 1864. That's when the Union army came through this neighborhood."

"How do you know?" said Eleanor, uncomfortable. She was glad Rachel liked the ghost, but she didn't want to think about him any more than she had to.

"It's on that historical marker by the Gas Town station. I've read books on it, too. There were tons of battles in Atlanta."

Rachel clicked her tongue. "That is so incredibly sad."

Charlie scooted forward enthusiastically. "You should have seen these soldiers. They must have been roasting! They had equipment hanging all over them—frying pans, bedrolls, guns, you name it. When they came to the pond, a bunch of them started throwing off their stuff. They jumped in so fast that they scared off a beaver."

Eleanor swallowed. She could almost see blue-coated young men, peeling off their hot jackets in her backyard.

"Did they"—Rachel bit her lip—"take off *all* their clothes?"

A blush spread over Charlie's cheeks. "Not everybody swam," he said, avoiding her question. "Some just picked the berries. Joseph got himself a tin cupful and sat down under that skinny oak tree. Your tree wasn't all that big back then," he explained to Eleanor.

Eleanor gazed out at her tree. Its gnarled old branches

sighed in the wind. It seemed impossible that in another time, a soldier boy had sat under it.

"What happened then?" asked Rachel.

"Not much at first," Charlie said. "An older man came and sat under the tree next to Joseph. They were just eating blackberries, watching the others swim.

"Then, all of a sudden, you could hear this cracking noise in the distance. Men started running through the woods. The man next to Joseph jumped up. 'Run, Joseph, run,' he yelled."

"Well," asked Rachel, "did he? Run, I mean?"

"You better believe he did. Ran clear out of sight. Then he came crashing back through the bushes—that's when you first saw him. He had forgotten his bugle, see."

"Poor guy!"

"Well, you've seen the rest. He blew his bugle and a bullet whizzed through the leaves and got him. It *was* pretty sad."

Rachel nodded slowly. "Very."

"I'll tell you one thing sadder, though."

Eleanor's mouth dropped open. Not something sadder!

"Soon, I'm afraid, we won't be able to see any of him."

Eleanor's first response was to jump for joy. She had had just about enough of Joseph. She stole a glance at Rachel.

Rachel actually looked unhappy. "Gosh, what can we do about it?" she said.

"Well, there is something we can do," said Charlie, looking at Eleanor.

Eleanor sighed. If only the ghost wasn't in *her* backyard. Had Joseph been anywhere else, she might have actually been glad to see him. Hadn't she always secretly wanted to be part of the past?

And now there was Rachel to think of, too. Rachel liked Joseph. And Rachel might be a way to get to Misty.

"All right," Eleanor sighed. "What do we have to do to keep him?"

Charlie spoke solemnly. "We've got to find more ways to connect him to the present."

⟦ 13 ⟧

Dem Bones

Eleanor could hardly concentrate on a word Charlie said. It wasn't the lunchroom noise that ruined her concentration, however. It was her location. After her disastrous party Friday, who would ever have thought that she would be sitting at Misty's table at lunch on Monday?

Okay, so she was at the end of the table, stuck across from Charlie. So she was eight people down from Misty. Misty probably didn't even know she was there. But for now, that was fine. She, Eleanor Cotton, was sitting at Misty's table!

When Eleanor first walked into the lunchroom that afternoon, she had thought Rachel was waving to someone else. Eleanor turned around to see who Rachel meant, but Rachel kept waving. Eleanor pointed to her chest. When Rachel nodded, Eleanor hurried over, thrilled, and not a little scared. Her excitement was dampened only slightly when Rachel waved Charlie over, too.

Now Rachel was leaning toward Charlie, her eyes squinted. "You really think that if there isn't stuff from the past still around"—she squinted her eyes even more —"Joseph *will go away?*"

Charlie took his usual collection of Baggies out of his paper sack. He spread them out in front of him in a row. "Right. Somehow, the past has to be connected to the present."

Eleanor was interested in what Charlie was saying, but she couldn't keep her eyes off Misty. Misty, on the other hand, was too busy talking and shaking her miniature troll doll earrings to notice.

"But I don't get it," Rachel protested. "If all it takes to connect ghosts like Joseph to the present is something from the past, then how come museums aren't full of ghosts?"

"Because the things from the past have to be at the same place where the people in the past used them," Charlie replied. "If the things get moved, the connection to the past is broken."

"How do you know all this?"

"I don't. But until I come up with something better— like I was telling you after Eleanor's party Friday, all we can do is try to find more ways to connect Joseph to the present."

Rachel wound her hair around her finger. "Okay,

okay. Let's think. What are the things connecting Joseph to Eleanor's yard?"

At the mention of her name, Eleanor pried her eyes off Misty. "What things in my yard?"

"Joseph's things," said Charlie. To Rachel, he said, "I guess the main thing that connects Joseph to Eleanor's yard is the tree. The pond's still there, too. I haven't noticed any blackberry bushes still around, have you, Eleanor?"

"Huh? Bushes? No." Her glance sidled back to Misty.

"I was thinking about this all weekend. You'd think"— Charlie chomped on a Chee-to—"you'd think that the bugle would be around somewhere, wouldn't you?"

"He did drop it after he got shot," Rachel agreed. "I saw that much."

At that moment, Misty turned in Eleanor's direction. Eleanor whirled around to face Charlie, her heart pounding. The last thing she needed was for Misty to catch her gawking.

"The bugle rolled down the hill," Eleanor said, heart still thumping. "Maybe it's still there."

She stole a glimpse of Misty. Misty was looking straight at her! And she was smiling, really smiling!

Eleanor ducked her head, glowing with private pleasure.

Next to her, Rachel shivered. "I just had an awful thought. Maybe Joseph's *bones* are still there. Maybe they just left him under Eleanor's tree. Wouldn't that be unbelievably sad!"

Eleanor stared open-mouthed, actually forgetting, for a second, about Misty. Bones? In her backyard? That was worse than a ghost!

Charlie smashed together an empty Baggie. "I never thought about bones! What a great idea!"

Rachel puffed with pride.

"You know what we've got to do, don't you?" Charlie's eyes shone.

"No," Eleanor said weakly.

"Dig!"

Eleanor gulped. "Dig?"

"Yes. Can we come over after school?"

Eleanor took a deep breath. She glanced at Misty, who was giggling as Nick reached for her dangly trolls. She turned to Rachel. "You coming, too?"

"Yes."

Eleanor let out her breath. "Come on over," Eleanor told Charlie.

⟦ 14 ⟧
The Pretenders

After school, Eleanor stood under the oak tree with Rachel and Charlie, staring at the ground. Though Charlie had a shovel, and Rachel and Eleanor each had one of Eleanor's mother's hand trowels, none of them had started digging. Eleanor was thinking about sleep. She knew she wouldn't be getting any. Nighttime and bones didn't mix.

"You think we ought to try to see Joseph one more time before we start digging?" Rachel asked at last.

"No!" exclaimed Eleanor. She cleared her throat. "I mean, no. I don't think that's polite, do you? Gawking at a guy, and then digging up his bones!"

The kitchen door opened. Buford rushed out to bound at Charlie's feet like a bucking bronco.

"Who let him out?" Eleanor yelled toward the house.

Audrey poked her head around the door and flashed a Pig.

"Call him back!" Eleanor bellowed.

"Oh, let him stay," said Charlie. "He can help dig."

Rachel hesitated. "Where do you think we should dig, Charlie?"

Charlie paced around the tree. He stopped next to an especially bumpy root. "How about right here?"

"You sure your mom won't mind?" Rachel asked Eleanor.

And chance putting a dent in her awkward daughter's social life? "Positive," said Eleanor.

Solemnly, Charlie put his shovel into the soil. He dug up a small scoop, and raised his eyebrows at the girls. They nodded again. He dug up another scoop, then another. Next to him, Buford began digging, too. Soon he was digging faster than Charlie, enthusiastically sending dirt flying behind him in a smooth orange arc.

Rachel dropped to her knees and pushed her beret back on her head. "Here goes nothing!" She chipped at the dirt, using her hand trowel like a dagger.

Eleanor took a big breath. Just how badly did she want to be Misty's friend? Normally, she wouldn't be caught dead digging up somebody's bones. Bones just weren't her style. And in her own backyard? . . . She wasn't going to sleep for *weeks*.

Yet, if she helped Rachel, and if she and Rachel got to be friends, well, that would put her one step closer to Misty. Maybe she wouldn't attract too much attention from Jessica that way, either. Sighing, she sat down cross-legged and gingerly scratched at the soil.

After a while, Buford trotted off to lie in the weeds by the pond. Rachel sat back on her heels. "Why do you think it is that Misty and those guys didn't see the ghost, Charlie?"

Charlie leaned on his shovel. "I think you have to have a feel for the past in order to see it. You have to believe in it. I guess they just didn't believe in it enough."

"I don't believe in ghosts," exclaimed Eleanor, "but I saw him!"

"I don't mean believing in *ghosts*. Joseph isn't like a regular ghost, anyhow. I mean believing in the past. That it was real. That it was here. That our time isn't the only time that ever existed."

"I believe in the past!" Rachel exclaimed. "I do! I think about it a lot. All those people, living and dying, living and dying—it's so *sad*."

Charlie nodded. "I know what you mean." They turned back to their digging.

"Okay, okay!" Before she could stop herself, Eleanor blurted out, "Sometimes I pretend I'm a pioneer girl!"

The others stopped digging. At last, Rachel said, "You do?"

Eleanor bit her lip. Why couldn't she keep her big mouth shut? No one pretended they were pioneers.

But Rachel just grinned. "Me, too!" she cried. "Sometimes I forget and I talk out loud. When I'm walking down the hall and people hear me say stuff like 'I'll make the porridge,' they really think I'm weird."

"Well, I pretend like I'm a soldier in the Civil War," Charlie admitted. "You think people look at *you* weird—you ought to see them when I dive for cover from an ambush!"

A smile grew on Eleanor's face. "You mean I'm not crazy when I pretend like I'm a pioneer?"

"No," said Charlie. "I think there are times when it's much more crazy *not* to pretend you're somebody else."

"Much more crazy," Rachel agreed.

"Really?" Eleanor sighed. She felt like she had just stepped out of a cast-iron suit. "I'm not nuts!" she murmured to herself. "I'm not nuts!"

"We ought to form a club," said Rachel.

"The Believers," Charlie suggested.

Eleanor shook her head. "That sounds too much like a church. How about . . . The Pretenders?"

"The Pretenders. I like it." Rachel raised her spade. "Fellow Pretenders: Dig!"

Charlie lifted his shovel. "Fellow Pretenders: Dig!" His shout brought Buford crashing out of the weeds.

"Fellow Pretenders: Dig!" echoed Eleanor. They banged their shovels together in a salute, and then pitched into the ground.

⟦ 15 ⟧
The Chain

Several hours and countless shovelfuls later, Eleanor stood knee-deep in an odd-shaped pit. She rubbed at her aching lower back. "If I hit one more root, I'm going to scream."

Rachel stopped chiseling at the side of the pit. She dropped her trowel and sadly studied the palms of her hands. "I think I've got blisters on my blisters."

"Well, Pretenders," said Charlie, laying his forehead on the end of his shovel handle, "I'm beginning to think somebody must have taken old Joseph away."

Rachel's eyes widened. "You mean, robbed his grave?"

"No. I mean took him away to bury him. Of course, you could be right. Somebody could have robbed his grave."

Rachel pulled her beret down over her ears. "Oooooo, sad!"

"Don't be gross!" said Eleanor quickly, trying to shut out pictures that would pester her for nights to come. "Nobody robbed Joseph's grave."

"You're right," said Charlie. "His bones were probably never here. Of course, if we had found his bones, that's what we would have been—grave robbers."

Eleanor moaned.

Rachel poked at her blisters. "So are we done digging?"

"What else could he have left behind?" Charlie said, kicking at the grass with his toe. "There has to be something else."

Eleanor pictured Joseph's hand flying to his chest. As the blood oozed between his fingers, something tumbled down the hill. "The bugle," she muttered.

Charlie snapped his fingers. "Right! Let's try digging for that!"

"I don't think I can," Rachel groaned.

Charlie paced down the hill to the edge of the road skirting the pond. "The way I figure it," he called over his shoulder, "the bugle rolled down here." He fell to his knees at the side of the road.

Eleanor and Rachel followed wearily. "It rolled down to the street?" Eleanor shouted.

Charlie tore at a chunk of grass on the hillside overhanging the road. "The road wasn't here in those days," he called back, not bothering to look up. "Tyler Drive is new. They put it in last summer when they built your house."

Charlie was scraping at the soil with his fingers when the girls arrived at the roadside. Suddenly, his arm sunk up to his elbow.

"What is it, Charlie?" asked Eleanor, half-afraid of the answer.

Charlie felt around in the hole. Suddenly, his arm froze. His eyes went wide.

Rachel gulped. "What is it?"

Sweat broke out on his forehead as he pulled at the thing in the ground. "I'm not sure. It's—"

The thing popped from the earth; Charlie fell on his back. From his fingers dangled a four-inch-long skinny object.

Eleanor squinted. "It looks like . . . a chain of some kind."

Charlie's face turned ghostly white. He swallowed loudly. "Have you ever seen that Civil War bugle at the Atlanta Historical Society?"

Eleanor shook her head.

"Well, it's got a little chain attached to the back of it. Just like this." He ran his hand through his hair, leaving it standing straight up. "It's supposed to keep the mouthpiece from getting lost."

Eleanor's mouth eased open as the importance of the

chain dawned upon her mind: There really was a bugle. There really was a Joseph. This was the chain to his bugle. Until now, she had seen, but even though she was a Pretender, had never really quite believed.

"Eleanor!" Mom called from the patio door. "Dinner!"

"Now?" yelled Eleanor, staring at the chain.

Mrs. Cotton stepped to the edge of the patio. "Would your friends like to stay and eat? You can have your own private picnic. You want to call home, Rachel and Charlie?"

Still reeling from Charlie's discovery, Eleanor waited on the patio as Charlie and Rachel called home. Minutes later, all three Pretenders seated themselves in thoughtful silence at the table. Buford stationed himself under the table for handouts.

"You do eat sloppy joes, don't you?" Mom asked Rachel as she whisked three plates of sloppy joes, complete with potato chips, in front of them. "The tomato sauce pretty well covers up the meat."

"Oh, sure," Rachel said, lifting her beret to scratch underneath it. "Thanks. I'll just pretend I'm eating a bunch of ketchup, not calves or cows or anything."

Mom blinked. "Good idea. Charlie? You don't have a problem with, uh, ketchup or calves, do you?"

"No, ma'am."

"Okay, then. Just call me if you need anything else!"

Eleanor blushed as her mother scampered into the house. It was embarrassing to have your mother even more anxious about your popularity than you are.

In her excitement about sitting at Misty's table that afternoon, Eleanor hadn't been able to eat much lunch. Now she was hungry. But Rachel and Charlie were busy talking. She couldn't go ahead and eat by herself and risk looking like a pig. It was rude. She would just have to wait. She fought against letting her gaze drift to the uneaten sloppy joes cooling on their plates as the sun slid below the neighboring pine trees.

"That's why Joseph's been fading," Charlie was saying. "Somebody took his bugle, and probably not that long ago, either. Don't you think the hole would have been filled in if the bugle had been gone very long? I'll bet somebody found it when they were putting in Tyler Drive."

"So now Joseph's mad," said Rachel.

"I don't think he's mad. He can't feel anything—mad, sad, whatever. He's stuck in the past."

Rachel nodded. "Oh, yeah. I forgot. But if he isn't mad, then why is losing his bugle making him fade away?"

"Because he's losing his connection through time. I thought you understood that."

Rachel wrinkled her nose. "Well, if that's the case, maybe you'd better put back the chain."

Charlie gasped. "You're right."

He seemed to see his sloppy joe for the first time. He scooped it up and took a big bite. Gratefully, Eleanor reached for her own. Her teeth were just sinking into the bun when Charlie said, his mouth half full, "Now we've really got to find that bugle."

Eleanor choked on her sloppy joe. This ghost thing had gone far enough. "Why?"

"How?" asked Rachel. She lifted the top of her sandwich and eyed the contents. Satisfied, she closed it and took a bite. "We'll never find"—she swallowed —"Joseph's bugle."

Charlie took a swig of Coke and wiped his face with the back of his hand. Then he smiled at Eleanor, which surprised her so much that she ducked her head in embarrassment. Her face had gone neon by the time he said, "Never say never!"

⟦ 16 ⟧
The Call

The next day, worry bubbled like molten lava in Eleanor's stomach as she shuffled along behind the boys' soccer team to the cafeteria. Lunchtime had always been the low point in her day at Sagamore, but today was worse than usual. Where was she supposed to sit?

Before making friends with Rachel, she had known her place, lowly as it was—Michael Pirkle's table. But now that Rachel had actually come to her house, was she supposed to sit with Rachel or act like they weren't friends? She didn't want to look too pushy, but on the other hand, she didn't want Rachel to think she was snubbing her.

It was all so hard! Why did Mr. Mandock have to call her to his desk after class just then to compliment her on her paper about the Renaissance? Eleanor was flattered that he wanted to talk to her about Michelangelo—

she loved Michelangelo—but Mr. Mandock's timing was terrible. If she could have left for lunch with the rest of the class, she could have weaseled in line next to Rachel. Maybe then Rachel would have invited her to sit with her at Misty's table. Things could have happened naturally, normally. But since when had anything natural and normal happened to Eleanor?

Now, as the soccer fanatics meandered toward their table, Eleanor had to make a choice. Should she go over to Misty's table and pray that Rachel would invite her to sit, or play it safe and park it next to Michael Pirkle?

Eleanor spotted Rachel. She was sitting at the edge of Misty's group, talking to Katherine. *She's forgotten me,* thought Eleanor. *She's got all her popular friends, why should she remember me?*

Eleanor stiffened. She had an even worse thought. Maybe Rachel thought she was weird! Maybe Rachel was only *pretending* she thought Joseph was cool. Maybe she was only *pretending* to pretend that she was a pioneer.

A-hilk! A-hilk! A-hilk! Jessica's laugh echoed across the cafeteria. Eleanor dared a peek out of the corner of her eye. Rachel was laughing, too! Could they be laughing at her? Could Rachel be entertaining the group with talk of how Eleanor and Charlie were actually digging for a ghost?

Sweating with embarrassment, Eleanor slithered into her customary seat. At the end of the table, the corners of Michael Pirkle's mouth were twitching in an attempt to smile. Only Michael Pirkle, eater of erasers, would want to be friends with her.

A lunch tray clattered on the table next to Eleanor. "Hi, Eleanor!" said Rachel. "You figure out how we're going to get that bugle yet?" She sat down and began poking at her Vegetarian Loaf as if nothing were wrong.

Tears of gratitude burned the back of Eleanor's throat. She had never expected Rachel to ever speak to her again.

Rachel cocked her head. "You okay?"

Eleanor nodded.

"Good. I've been thinking—oh hey, there's Charlie."

Charlie sat down across from Eleanor with his paper bag.

"I've been thinking," Rachel began again earnestly. "I think we should look into getting some blackberry bushes." She smiled apologetically at Charlie. "Just in case we don't find the bugle, that is. If we plant some blackberry bushes, maybe Joseph will—"

"Don't look now," hissed Eleanor, "but Misty's looking!"

Eleanor couldn't believe what happened next. Rachel leaned back and waved! From Michael Pirkle's table, Rachel had the nerve to wave!

Sweet as usual, Misty waved back.

"Wave, Eleanor," said Rachel.

Eleanor raised her hand to her chin and waggled her fingers timidly.

Just then, Jessica turned around. Eleanor's fingers froze in mid-waggle. Jessica's lips curled up in a snarl.

Eleanor slunk back around like a whipped puppy. Had Jessica singled her out as somebody who was especially despicable, or did Jessica just hate everybody? "What did I do?" she groaned out loud.

Charlie stopped talking about blackberry bushes. "What?"

"Nothing. It's just that . . . Jessica hates me." Embarrassed, Eleanor let her voice trail off.

"Aw, Jessica's hated everybody since kindergarten," said Charlie. "Don't pay any attention to her."

Rachel snorted. "That's kind of impossible, Charlie. If Jessica's got it in for you, she's a lit-tle hard to ignore. Want me to tell her to stuff it, Eleanor?"

Eleanor's mouth hung open in horror. Jessica—stuffing it? You just don't tell people like Jessica to stuff it. And what if Jessica found out who Rachel was telling her to stuff it for?

"No," said Eleanor quickly. "No, please!"

Rachel shrugged. The rest of lunchtime, while Rachel and Charlie talked about Joseph, Eleanor worried.

So Rachel didn't deny it. Jessica had it in for her. Why? What had she done? Did Jessica hate all new girls, or just her? And what did Jessica do to people she had it in for? Just snarl and threaten . . . or something really bad?

"Eleanor, are you listening?" said Rachel.

"What? . . . Yes." Eleanor noticed that Rachel's Vegetarian Loaf was already almost eaten. Her own lunch tray was still untouched.

"Well," asked Rachel, "what do you think of Charlie doing some more digging after school while we call up different antique places?"

"Antique places? What happened to the blackberry bushes?"

"You weren't listening. We decided to go after the bugle. We know it's out there. We're going to call antique stores in case one of them has it. And Charlie wants to keep digging in case Joseph left more stuff."

"Oh. Okay."

"Charlie and I will ride our buses home, and then come right over on our bikes, okay?"

Eleanor bit her lip. Maybe it wasn't healthy having Rachel over. Maybe it would make Jessica mad. After all, Rachel was part of Misty's group.

On the other hand, Eleanor thought, Rachel had been nice enough to sit with her at lunch. Besides Charlie— and Michael Pirkle—Rachel was the only person at Sagamore who took her seriously. Rachel was loyal, and fun, too. It wouldn't be nice just to drop her. In fact, it would be plain stupid.

"Okay," Eleanor sighed.

"Good. We'll be over after school."

Heavy-hearted, Eleanor went through the trash line.

As she dumped the untouched contents of her tray into the yellow trash bin, she almost cried. She had gotten used to the idea of not being thought of as cute and funny. She had gotten used to the idea of not being popular. She had even gotten used to the idea of sitting at Michael Pirkle's table for the rest of her life. That wasn't so bad now that Rachel was sitting with her. But would she ever, ever, get used to the idea of being despised by Jessica Grenzig?

*

After school, Eleanor paced the sidewalk, waiting for Audrey. It was bad enough that she had to walk the brat home, but being stuck at school one more second longer than she had to be was sheer torture. Standing on the sidewalk in front of the school, she felt exposed and alone—a single elephant on an open plain surrounded by hunters with elephant guns.

Nick and Theo burst out of the building. Eleanor turned away, cringing. She could hear them shoving and laughing their way through a crowd of fourth graders. She edged toward some bushes, hoping to blend in.

"Hey, there's Eleanor!" cried Nick.

Bang! The elephant fell.

"Hey, Eleanor!" Nick ran by her backward. "WooOooOooooo! Where's the ghost?"

Theo warbled, "I think I see spirits!" They turned and ran, laughing, to their bus.

Eleanor hung her head. Joseph could be as real as the President of the United States—still, she was never going to live down that party.

She heard a faint tapping sound. Nick and Theo grinned at her from the back window of their bus.

At least Misty wasn't around to see them, Eleanor comforted herself. Misty's mother had already picked Misty up in her car, as soon as they got out of school.

Audrey skipped up, wearing a boy's red jacket. "Like my coat? It's Tyler's." She modeled it by flapping it open and closed.

"Give it back," Eleanor growled. "Hurry!" She started walking.

"Tyler says he's going to bring me something real neat soon," said Audrey, skipping after her. "Something valuable."

"Right. A diamond ring."

"You don't believe me, just see what—"

"Would you shut up?" Eleanor cried. "Give Tyler back his coat and hurry up! I'm not waiting. I've got company coming."

Audrey skipped back to Tyler, but Eleanor didn't slow her pace. Let Tyler walk Audrey home, if he loved her that much.

"Eleanor, wait!" Audrey called.

Eleanor started running. It felt good, making her legs pump and her heart pound.

"Eleanor, please wait!"

Hearing her popular sister beg felt even better. Of course Eleanor would let her catch up, but Audrey didn't have to know that.

They ran neck to neck all the way home. Panting, they staggered into the kitchen. The phone rang.

The calls were never for her since she had moved to Sagamore, but Eleanor picked up the receiver out of deeply ingrained habit. "Hello?"

"Hello? Eleanor? This is Misty."

Eleanor now knew what it meant to be so surprised that you drop your teeth. She actually had to push her jaw back in place with her fingers. "Yes?"

"Well, I was wondering if you'd like to come over to my house."

All the basic questions jammed up in Eleanor's mind. Who? What? Why? Where? When? She picked one. "When?" she squeaked.

"Now."

"Now?"

"Unless you've got something else you've got to do."

"No! I can come!"

"Great! Come right away, then. Do you know where I live?"

Eleanor did. During the last few weeks, she had made her mother drive past Misty's house several times. "I'll get my mom to bring me," she said.

"Good. See you soon."

"What's with you?" Audrey called after Eleanor as

Eleanor danced down the hall and up the stairs. She waltzed over to her bed without the slightest thought of ghosts, and then swan-dived onto the covers. Buford awoke with a jingle of tags in his corner.

Suddenly Eleanor remembered: Rachel. Her joy popped as quickly as a balloon on a pricker bush. She limped down to the kitchen and dialed Rachel's number from the school directory.

"Rachel? Hi, this is Eleanor. About this afternoon—I have to cancel. I have"—Eleanor flinched, hating to lie—"to go shopping with my mother."

"Do you have to go today? We're so close to finding Joseph's bugle."

Eleanor swallowed. "I have to. I guess there's . . . some sale."

"Oh, man."

Eleanor felt miserable, but she couldn't stop now. "Could you call Charlie, and tell him for me?"

"Okay. See you tomorrow."

Eleanor hung up, feeling like scum. Rachel had sat with her at lunch. She had called Eleanor over to Misty's table after the flop of the Friday the thirteenth party. She had even wanted to be friends after Eleanor had admitted that she pretended she was a pioneer girl.

But still—Misty wanted her! Who wouldn't go over to Misty's if Misty had called them? Being Misty's buddy was her dream!

She dug her magazine out from under her pillow. She turned to the article about popularity. With her finger, she skimmed down the paragraphs. There it was, in black and white: *Don't* give up. *Do* be creative. According to the article, she was *supposed* to go to Misty's.

Rachel would understand, wouldn't she?

⟦ 17 ⟧
Secret Twins

Eleanor sat on Misty's bed, in Misty's room, pretending to play with one of Misty's stuffed animals, a tiger kitten. Eleanor petted the kitten and even retied the silky red ribbon around its neck, but she wasn't really playing with it. What Eleanor was really doing was taking a mental picture.

Not long ago, Mrs. Leto had taught Eleanor's class how to take a mental picture. A person takes a mental picture, Mrs. Leto had told them, when she concentrates on what's around her. A person needs to tune into details and, more important, use all of her five senses. "If you want to remember something for the rest of your life," Mrs. Leto promised, "then taking a mental picture will do it."

Making it to Misty's house was something Eleanor

definitely wanted to remember forever. Replaying a good mental picture of the occasion would be better than watching TV! Eleanor would get in all five senses if it killed her.

So far, the sense-of-touch part was easy. As Misty dug through her box of tapes on the other side of the room, Eleanor stroked the stuffed tiger until she was sure that for the rest of her life, whenever she touched a fuzzy toy, she would instantly think of this moment.

Getting in the sense of sight was simple, too. All Eleanor had to do was to use her eyes like a camera.

Misty pawed through her tapes. Click.

Misty tossed back her silver-blond hair. Click.

Misty's triangle earrings twirled like little tops. Click.

Misty lifted her finger and flicked at the inside of her nose.

Eleanor decided to move on to her sense of hearing. She squeezed her eyes shut and listened. There was the clacking sound of the tapes being shuffled in their box. Downstairs, someone turned a TV on, adding its babble to the background. Now Misty sniffed, three short times. Silence.

Eleanor's attention wandered. She was trying to think of the other two senses.

Her eyes opened with a frown. She remembered now. She certainly didn't know how she could taste Misty's room. And as for smelling—

Misty stood up, causing her earrings to go wild. "Who do you like best—R.A.D. or Moon Tiger?" She held up two tapes.

Eleanor froze in the middle of her mental picture. Since she had arrived at Misty's, things had been going better than her wildest dreams. She'd had a snack of cookies and milk and not spilled anything down her front. She hadn't burped. She hadn't said anything dumb. Actually, to be safe, she hadn't said much of anything. And now Misty was asking a question that just might trip her up for good.

Eleanor thought fast. Which group would Misty like? R.A.D. was loud and raunchy. Eleanor's mother turned the radio off whenever she was in Eleanor's room and they came on, a point in their favor.

On the other hand, Moon Tiger consisted of two girls who sang very high. They sounded the way Misty might sound, if she sang.

Eleanor took a chance. "Moon Tiger."

"Wow!" Misty exclaimed as she jammed the Moon Tiger tape into the tape player. "Me, too! I don't really like R.A.D. that much, but Jessica got it for me for my birthday."

The mention of Jessica made Eleanor squirm. She decided to risk talking in order to divert the subject. "So, um, when's your birthday?"

Misty shook back her hair. "August fifteenth."

"Really?" Eleanor blinked. "Mine's August sixteenth!"

Misty's mouth dropped open. "You're kidding! We're practically twins!"

Eleanor beamed. Dumpy little butter-blond her, Misty's twin? Oh, this was definitely a day to remember!

"So what's your favorite color, Twin?" said Misty, sitting cross-legged next to Eleanor on the bed.

Eleanor gazed around Misty's room, her heart beating fast. The curtains were pink, the walls were pink, the bedspread was pink. Though Eleanor's own favorite color was aqua, she guessed that wasn't the right answer.

"Pink," she said.

"This is unbelievable—*mine too!*"

Eleanor couldn't have glowed more if she were a lightning bug. She let herself sway to the sweet voices of Moon Tiger.

"Have you written any more toilet paper notes lately?" asked Misty, throwing her hair over her shoulder.

Eleanor stared at one of Misty's triangle earrings. She would not let the memory of the toilet paper disaster ruin this wonderful moment. "No. Not lately."

"Too bad. Those were funny. Getting them wet was a hilarious idea. Real authentic!"

Eleanor stole a sidelong glance. Misty didn't *look* like she was making fun.

"Jessica and those guys should have never torn them up," Misty continued. "They were so funny! Eleanor, you are hilarious."

"I am?"

"I thought I was going to die when you said 'Bob Hope' instead of 'the pope' in Mandock's class."

"You did?"

"Are you kidding? Nobody else would have had the nerve. Mandock's got everybody freaked. They must really miss you at your old school. What was it like, anyways?"

With a pang, Eleanor thought of Susan. Then she thought of Susan, hanging around with Ant Brain Lorraine. "Not so great."

"Oh, too bad." Misty flicked her silvery hair over her shoulders. "You want another snack?"

Though Eleanor was too nervous to be hungry, she nodded.

"Peanut butter on celery or Honey Pops cereal?"

Eleanor sighed. At least, if they ate, they wouldn't talk. And the less they talked, the less chance Eleanor had of sounding ridiculous. "Can we have both?" she asked, not knowing which snack to choose.

"That's what I was going to say!" Misty exclaimed. "We really are twins, you know it?" Her silver laugh tinkled like wind chimes.

Eleanor smiled wanly.

Down in the kitchen, Misty handed Eleanor four stalks of celery, a jar of peanut butter, and a knife. "You fix these, and I'll get the cereal."

Eleanor nodded. She set the celery on the counter.

She aimed a knifeful of peanut butter into the center of the celery, but the stalk rocked like a miniature boat. The peanut butter blobbed all over the sides. Klutz! She snuck a peek at Misty. Not a single Honey Pop bounced onto the floor as she poured the cereal into the bowl. Buford would starve around here, Eleanor said to herself.

"Honey Pops are my favorite cereal," said Misty. "What's yours?"

Eleanor looked up guiltily from the mess she was making of the celery. At least she knew the right answer. "Honey Pops."

Misty nodded serenely, as if she had already guessed the answer. She got the milk from the refrigerator and neatly poured it over the cereal. "What's something cool they used to do at your old school?" she asked, putting away the milk.

"Well, Spirit Days were kind of cool." Eleanor frowned at her fingers, which were now webbed together with peanut butter.

"What're Spirit Days?"

"Every week, Student Council made Friday a certain kind of day. On Hat Day, everyone was supposed to wear hats. On Braves Day, everyone's supposed to wear Braves junk. On Nerd Day, you were supposed to dress nerdy."

"That sounds great! We should do that at Sagamore."

Sadly, Eleanor remembered her favorite Spirit Day of

all. Twin Day. She and Susan used to go to a lot of detail, planning their twin outfits. They even went so far as to wear the same color underwear, lilac.

Ant Brain Lorraine wanted to make them triplets, but Susan wouldn't let her. Susan wanted it to be just her and Eleanor, marching into class in their matching red-and-white-striped sweaters and black pants. Good old Susan. Eleanor sighed. "Twin Day was kind of fun."

"Yeah? What was that?"

"When you and a friend come to school dressed alike."

Misty cleared her throat. "Um, Eleanor, one thing about us being twins . . ."

"Yes?" Eleanor hoped Misty didn't see her wipe her peanut-buttery fingers on her jeans.

". . . well, we've kind of got to keep it secret."

Eleanor bit her lip. She thought about Twin Day with Susan. Wasn't that the object of being twins—showing off who was your buddy? "Okay," she said slowly.

"In fact, you had better not tell anyone you were here at all. You do understand, don't you? It's Jessica. She can be such a pain sometimes. She thinks she owns me, but she doesn't."

Misty took two of the peanut butter celerys and headed for the table. "Grab a couple napkins from that napkin holder there. This celery is a mess."

Eleanor grabbed the napkins and numbly followed Misty to the table.

Misty smiled encouragingly. "Anyhow, don't you think being *secret* twins is more fun? We can have our own secret sign. How about that funny face you made— you know, by flipping back your eyelids?"

Eleanor sucked in her breath. She'd hoped the Pig Face would die quietly.

"Naaa," said Misty, "that face takes too long. Let's just wink. Whenever I wink at you, you wink back. It's the Sign of the Twins. Now, wink."

Misty started winking so crazily that Eleanor had to laugh. "Twins for life?" Misty asked, still winking.

Eleanor smiled hopefully. "Twins for life."

⟦ 18 ⟧

Phone Order Ghost

Eleanor sat in homeroom and fiddled with the zipper on her backpack. Ever since Misty had walked into homeroom ten minutes ago, she had been a nervous wreck. Should she look at Misty and give her their secret wink, or should she play it safe and ignore her?

All last night, Eleanor had worried. She'd had a hard time falling asleep, wondering if Misty had made up the idea of being secret twins just to be nice. Eleanor was afraid it was like when she told Ant Brain Lorraine that next time there was a Twin Day, she could be a triplet. Eleanor hadn't meant that for a minute. She was only trying to make Ant Brain feel better.

Actually, Eleanor thought now, zipping the zipper back and forth, ol' Ant Brain hadn't been so bad. Though she was too much of an eager beaver, and had all the grace of a cow, Ant Brain had been fun. No one made Susan and Eleanor laugh the way Ant Brain did.

It was just that, last year, whenever Susan started spending a lot of time with Ant Brain, Eleanor had felt weird. A green, almost burpy feeling started in Eleanor's stomach, and worked its way up to her throat. Sometimes, Eleanor felt as if she could almost choke on it. But Eleanor would have never called herself jealous. Annoyed, maybe, but not jealous. Not like Jessica.

"Who's buying lunch today?" Mrs. Leto asked. "Let's have a hand count, please."

Eleanor raised her hand but kept her gaze on her backpack. She tugged at the zipper. Zip! Zip!

"Now who wants salads?" asked Mrs. Leto.

Eleanor could feel hands raising around her, but didn't dare look. Misty usually ordered a salad.

Zip! Zip!

"Jumbo lunches?" asked Mrs. Leto.

Eleanor knew no one would be raising hands now. No one ever ordered a jumbo lunch. Nobody had the nerve.

Zip!

"Whoever's playing with the zipper, please stop it," said Mrs. Leto, not looking up from where she was jotting down the lunch count at her desk.

Eleanor froze. She could feel eyes upon her. Her hands crawled into her lap.

The first few notes of "The Star-spangled Banner"

blared over the P.A. Eleanor struggled to her feet and put her hand over her chest. All around her, sleepy voices began murmuring to the music.

Under her hand, Eleanor's heart thumped like a scared rabbit's. Now was the perfect time to steal a glance at Misty—now, while everybody was so embarrassed to be singing that they were afraid to look around.

First she moved her eyes, all the way to the sides of their sockets. Then, when her eye muscles groaned in pain, she gave her head a jerk. Her glance connected with Misty. Misty was winking!

Eleanor nearly hugged herself. Misty and she were really friends! She glowed through the rest of "The Star-spangled Banner."

"Okay, line up for social studies, gang," said Mrs. Leto.

Eleanor stole another look at Misty as she gathered up her books. Misty glanced up just in time for Eleanor to give her a wink.

"Got something in your eye?" Rachel asked, stopping beside Eleanor.

"No," said Eleanor quickly. "I mean, yes." Eleanor's shoulders almost twitched with guilt.

Rachel frowned. "Missed you last night."

"M'mmm."

"Charlie ended up coming over to my house. We called a whole bunch of antique stores on the phone. Nobody had any bugles. One guy even thought we were kidding around. He said we better not ask if his refrigerator was running, because he wasn't going to catch it."

Eleanor laughed uneasily. She wished she hadn't lied about going over to Misty's yesterday. And now she could never tell where she'd been—she had promised Misty she wouldn't. What was it about being Misty's secret twin that made Eleanor so uncomfortable around Rachel? Rachel wouldn't care, Eleanor told herself. Rachel was too busy dreaming about pioneers and dead soldiers.

"I don't think calling antique shops is going to get us anywhere," Rachel said. "We need to dig some more, see what else we can find. How about if Charlie and I come over after school today?" Rachel frowned. "Or do you think your mom will make you go shopping again?"

"Oh no! No! No shopping! We're done."

Rachel scratched under her beret. "What, don't you like shopping?"

Eleanor pretended not to hear.

"Anyway," said Rachel, "let's dig, huh?"

"What—dig? Oh, yeah, sure."

"Good, I'll go ask Charlie."

Eleanor walked into Mr. Mandock's room alone. Suddenly, she was reminded of the dream that had awakened her in the night. In her dream, she was walking up to the pencil sharpener in Mr. Mandock's room. She was trying to catch Misty's eye in a secret wink. But Misty turned away, laughing. Soon the whole class was laughing. Eleanor looked down. She had on shoes, and white

119

socks. Other than that, nothing. She was naked to the world.

Just remembering the dream made Eleanor break out in a sweat. She glanced down quickly. Relief poured through her veins like water. Clothes! Her old red-and-white-striped sweater had never looked so good.

Misty returned Eleanor's wink exactly five and a half times that day (one of the winks had been cut short when Jessica looked up). Even so, after school it was a relief to be home. From all the dashing and darting they had done that day, Eleanor's eyes actually ached. From worrying about Jessica catching her, the whole back of her head throbbed, too. What a relief to be back with Rachel, on the ground, on her knees, digging into the hard dirt around the roots of the oak tree. It even felt good, she admitted begrudgingly, to be with Charlie.

Halfway around the tree, Charlie exclaimed, "Get down, Buford! How am I supposed to dig when you're jumping on me?"

Eleanor stopped digging. Buford was springing at Charlie's face, his tongue darting out like an anteater's. For the first time that day, Eleanor laughed out loud.

"Buford, get down!" she ordered, trying unsuccessfully to sound masterful.

Hearing his name, Buford stopped jumping. He cocked his ears hopefully.

"Buford, lie down!"

Buford bounded over to Eleanor, overjoyed. He circled around her happily, taking swipes at her chin, thrashing her with his tail.

"Your breath stinks! Get down!"

Filled with love, Buford licked and lunged.

Just then, Rachel gasped. "Oh, my gosh!"

"Buford, quit!" Eleanor stuck out an elbow. "What is it, Rachel?"

Rachel drew in her breath. "A bone." Solemnly, she held up the evidence.

Eleanor dropped her hand trowel and rushed over. Charlie ran to her, too, but Buford was faster. With a single lunge, he snatched the bone out of Rachel's hand and peeled toward the pond.

"Catch him!" Charlie yelled. "It might be Joseph!"

Rachel covered her face. "Oh, *sad!*"

Eleanor and Charlie raced after Buford. Buford ran to the pond, seemed to consider jumping in, then doubled back. He darted toward Eleanor and Charlie, then wheeled away, but not quickly enough. Charlie and Eleanor sprang on him at the same time. They landed in a tangle.

Eleanor snatched the bone from Buford's mouth. "Got it!"

Suddenly, Eleanor was aware of Charlie's legs and arms against hers. She leaped up, embarrassed.

Charlie got slowly to his feet. He was pinker than Buford's tongue. "Let me see that bone," he mumbled.

Eleanor handed him the bone, embarrassingly conscious of the places on her arms and legs where Charlie had brushed against her.

"This isn't Joseph," said Charlie.

Eleanor tried to focus in on the bone. "It's not?"

"No. It's a T-bone. Like from a steak." He held up the bone. It was actually shaped like a T.

"Buford must have buried it," Eleanor muttered.

Rachel trotted up. "You mean that's not Joseph?"

"No."

"Phew! I just can't think of Joseph as a *bone*."

"At least not a T-bone," Charlie agreed.

"I want to see him again," said Rachel. "I want to remember him like he was." She shivered. "I just keep picturing *steaks*."

"Well, I'm going to try and see him," said Charlie. He stalked toward the tree.

"Are you okay, Eleanor?" Rachel asked.

"Yes. I'm perfectly fine," Eleanor said firmly. She wobbled over to the tree where Charlie, still pink around the ears, appeared to be studying something in the distance.

"Okay," said Rachel, "close your eyes. Concentrate hard as you can."

Eleanor closed her eyes. Immediately, the air began to hum. The air grew so heavy it seemed to weigh on the hairs of her arms. Suddenly, Joseph's image shimmered into view. He was holding his chest. Blood oozed.

The bugle rolled down the hill. The picture dissolved. Eleanor opened her eyes.

"Wow, was that fast!" exclaimed Rachel.

"There's not much left, is there?" To Eleanor's surprise, she felt disappointed.

"We've got to do something," said Charlie, "quick. He's almost gone."

Eleanor surveyed the yard. It looked like a battlefield, but not from the Civil War. The craters all around her were brand new. "Somehow," she said, "I don't think digging is helping."

"He likes it." Rachel nodded toward Buford, who was starting in on a new hole.

"Digging's no good," Charlie admitted. "Antique stores are out, too. What are we going to do?"

Charlie looked so sad, Eleanor couldn't stand it. "Well," she said after a minute, "what about getting a blackberry bush, like Rachel said? We can plant it near the tree, just like in Joseph's time."

Charlie's brows lifted with gratitude. "You think your mom would mind?"

Eleanor almost laughed. Her mom would let them plant poison ivy if she thought it would help Eleanor with her friends. "I don't think so," she said.

"Do you know of any blackberry bushes in the neighborhood?" Rachel asked Charlie.

"No. And with their leaves starting to fall off, I don't think I'd know one if I saw one."

"We can call a plant nursery," offered Eleanor. "If they have them at Green's, we could ride over on our bikes and get one."

"I've got to go to my piano lesson in a few minutes," said Rachel, "but I can go with you guys tomorrow."

They ran into the house and got out the phone book. Standing close to Charlie, Eleanor suddenly felt so shy that she wanted to kick herself. Shy, around an egghead! She forced herself to sound normal. "You call, Charlie," she said. "You sound more professional."

Charlie's eyebrows went up. His face flashed red. "Really?"

Eleanor handed him the receiver.

"Yes," Charlie said into the phone. His voice was as low and firm as a TV announcer's. "Do you carry blackberry bushes?"

There was a pause.

"You do?" he squeaked. He lowered his voice. "You do. And how much are they? Five ninety-five?" He raised his eyebrows at Eleanor and Rachel. They nodded.

"Well, could you please hold one until tomorrow? The name is Ormsby. Charles Ormsby."

Eleanor grinned, in spite of the fact that, basically, she was helping Charlie order up a ghost. She opened up the refrigerator. "Anyone want a snack?"

⟦ 19 ⟧
The Love Note

Immediately after Rachel and Charlie left, Eleanor dumped the contents of her miniature white garbage can on the bed and began sorting it into piles. A pile of dimes to the left, a pile of quarters to the right, a very short stack (two) of crumpled bills in the middle. She straightened the bills against her leg. Both of them would have to go toward the blackberry bush. Eleanor thought of Joseph eating blackberries under her tree back in 1864, a bugle boy far from home. She guessed he was worth it.

The phone rang. "Get it, somebody," Eleanor yelled. Buford stirred in the corner, but the rest of the house was silent.

"Get—" Eleanor broke off. Her mother was at the grocery store; Dad was at the Pizza Station; her darling sister was at a friend's house; Ben was out being Ben somewhere. She lunged for the phone. "Hullo?"

A silvery voice tinkled over the phone. "Hi, Twin!"

A funny feeling nudged Eleanor's gut. Nerves, she decided. "Hi, Twin."

"I just ditched Jessica, and I'm about to go crazy over here. My mom cleaned all the carpets in the house. Everywhere you walk it's sopping wet. I'm marooned on my bed—my socks are gross."

An opportunity from heaven! She had to be brave. She cleared her throat and braced herself for rejection. "Want to come over here?"

"Lord, yes!" Misty's laugh reminded Eleanor of tinsel on Christmas trees. "I'll get my mom to bring me."

"Great!"

But when Eleanor hung up, she realized things weren't so great. The house was a pit! She started shoving things under her bed. Clothes and shoes flew toward the closet. Her little wicker wastebasket toppled under a heap of old school papers.

Eleanor slapped her hand over her mouth. "Oh my gosh—the kitchen!" She raced downstairs with Buford jingling after her.

After a quick run through the family room (newspapers and the open Clue game swept under the couch, Dad's slippers popped into the magazine basket), she tackled the kitchen.

"Buford—here!" Eleanor tossed two slices of bread into the air. Buford snatched them before they hit the floor. His eyes brightened.

"Cookie?" Without looking, Eleanor tossed half an Oreo and some potato chips over her shoulder. The snapping of dog jaws satisfied her that the job was getting done.

She began flinging the cups and bowls on the counter into the sink like so many Frisbees. She paused on a bowl puddled with melted chocolate ice cream: Charlie's bowl. She stared at it reverently.

Don't be ridiculous! she scolded herself.

She dropped the dish into the sink.

She was running a wet dishcloth down the counter when the doorbell rang. She sprinted to the door, combing her sticky fingers through her hair. A dream was coming true—Misty was coming to visit!

Misty stood in the door, eyeing Buford. "My gosh, I'd forgotten how big he is."

"He's really pretty sweet," said Eleanor, trying to lug Buford back from the door. "He just looks big."

Misty wrinkled her nose. "*Smells* big too!"

"So," said Eleanor, after she had locked Buford in the bathroom and Misty had followed her up to her room, "what do you want to do?" She stood by the door, shoulders tensed, arms clamped over her chest. You're supposed to be having fun, she reminded herself.

"I don't know." Misty tossed back her hair. "What do you usually do?"

What Eleanor usually did these days was chase ghosts, but she knew exactly how that would sound to Misty. It sounded that way to her, too. She tried to remember what she used to do with Susan. In her panic, she could only think of one thing. "Um," she said in a squeaky little voice that was definitely not hers, "you want to make toilet paper notes?"

"Us?"

Eleanor cringed. Why was she such a dunce?

"Great!" said Misty. "Do you have enough toilet paper?"

"Lots!"

Eleanor almost skipped to the bathroom. This was just like old times, when she and Susan used to team up and write t.p. notes for all the cool kids in class! She dug into the bathroom closet, joyously knocking over old bottles of medicine and shampoo before she found an extra roll of toilet paper.

Eleanor perched on the bed next to Misty. "Here's the paper. Who should we make them to?"

"I want to make one for Jessica."

Eleanor shot her a look.

Misty put her hand to her lips. "Oops! Bad idea, bad idea. Though it would have been funny to pretend it was from Theo. She's just so sure he's in love with her."

Eleanor shifted uncomfortably. Who were they going to make the notes for? If they made them for any of the girls in Misty's group, they might tell Jessica. Except Rachel. Rachel wouldn't tell, Eleanor thought guiltily.

"I've got an idea," said Misty.

"What?"

"Michael Pirkle."

Eleanor frowned. "Michael Pirkle?"

"Yes. Let's give him one."

Someone like Michael Pirkle could never appreciate a good t.p. note, Eleanor was sure. He'd probably eat it. "Why would we give him a letter?"

"As a joke, get it? We'll say that one of us loves him."

"Which one of us?"

Misty tossed her hair. "You."

Eleanor thought of Michael's pathetic little half smiles at lunch. Picking on him was like picking on a kitten. It wasn't even funny.

"I don't think that's such a good idea."

"Why not? He'll think it's funny!" Misty took the red marker from the table by Eleanor's bed and wrote "To My Lover" at the top of a long piece of toilet paper.

"I have to sit by him at lunch," said Eleanor, watching Misty write.

"I've been meaning to tell you—you really shouldn't sit there. Jessica's been talking about it. I just hate to hear her talk so ugly!"

Eleanor scowled. "What's she say?"

"She says it's bad enough that you and Charlie have a thing going—"

"We do not!" Eleanor broke in.

"—but sitting next to Michael Pirkle makes you look like a 'total turkey.' She said it, not me."

"Charlie and I do not have anything going," Eleanor repeated.

"Oh, I know that! A twin of mine would have better taste."

Eleanor blinked. The fact was, Charlie wasn't so bad. He was almost even cute. . . . "Rachel sits by Michael and Charlie," she said aloud.

Misty tossed her hands. "Rachel is Rachel. Nobody can do anything with her. She's a free spirit. Kind of a *sad* free spirit, if you know what I mean, but a free spirit."

Eleanor watched as Misty wrote some more. A definite funny feeling was nudging her in her gut.

"Anyhow," said Misty, not looking up, "come sit by me at lunch."

Eleanor inhaled sharply. "What about Jessica?"

Misty looked up. "You're right. I don't know what to do about her. She's so mean to all my friends! I know I should ditch her, but I just can't. You understand, don't you?"

Eleanor nodded. She didn't understand at all.

Misty bent over her writing. After a minute, she said,

"Listen to this: 'I have been in love with you ever since the moment I laid eyes on you. Do you love me, too? If you do, check one of these boxes. Yes. No. Maybe.'" She turned the wispy length of paper around for Eleanor to sign. "Michael's going to have a cow!"

Hesitantly, Eleanor took the red marker. "Maybe you should sign this, Misty. I mean, you're so pretty and everything. It won't mean anything to him if he gets this from me."

"I can't. I've known Michael Pirkle since kindergarten. He knows I can't stand him. Here, sign."

Eleanor took a deep breath, and then scribbled her name. On the *r*, the tip of her pen tore a hole in the toilet paper.

"Now don't tell anyone that we wrote this," Misty said. "This is *our* secret."

Eleanor nodded. Somehow, that suited her fine. "What am I supposed to do with it?" she said miserably.

"Stick it in his desk before school starts tomorrow. That ought to make his day!"

[20]

Puppy Dog Eyes

Audrey skipped along next to Eleanor as they walked to school the next morning. She'd been singing "If You're Happy and You Know It" since they had left home. Eleanor watched her sister through slitted eyes. She was definitely not happy, and furthermore, she knew it. Her mood matched the low gray clouds overhead. The morning promised rain.

Audrey finished her song and cartwheeled into the grass by the sidewalk. "Today's the big day!" she exclaimed.

Panic zapped through Eleanor like a bolt of lightning. She lunged forward and grabbed Audrey by the arm. "What do you mean, 'Today's the big day'? Who told you today's the big day?"

Audrey shook free. "Today's the day Tyler's bringing me my big surprise. What's the matter with you?"

"I thought you were talking about something else," Eleanor muttered. She shifted under the straps of her backpack. Inside the backpack, under the jacket her mother had forced her to take, under her math book, under her science book, under her social studies book, the toilet paper love note for Michael Pirkle waited like something live.

It was like in one of those horror movies where something innocent like a glob of goo or a harmless housefly grows into a monster. Eleanor had visions of the t.p. note stirring to life. First it would taste her science book. Then it would munch her math book. It would keep on gobbling and growing, gobbling and growing, until soon it would spill out, huge, onto the sidewalk . . .

"Maybe he'll give me a gerbil," said Audrey. "Tyler knows I like animals. I'd take a hamster, too. Do you think Mom would—"

"Like I really care what Tyler's giving you! Audrey, would you just shut up?"

The hurt expression on Audrey's face made Eleanor feel even worse. She looked down at her hands. To her dismay, they were shaking. She glanced up at Audrey, who was regarding her solemnly.

"What are you staring at?"

"You. You look weird. You sad or something?"

Eleanor opened her mouth to snarl a reply, but nothing came out. In a flash of memory, Audrey was standing before her as a toddler. Wispy-haired and dressed in overalls, she gazed at Eleanor in wide-eyed wonder. Eleanor had just showed her how to climb out of her crib. Audrey had looked so appreciative and surprised that Eleanor couldn't help it: She had squeezed Audrey so tight that it made both of them grunt.

"You okay?"

Eleanor blinked. The spell was broken. "Yeah, sure I'm okay."

Of course she was okay. She was Misty's secret twin. She wiped the tears that had sprung to her eyes on her sleeve, and ran ahead alone. Her heart felt as sore as a bruise.

Eleanor arrived in front of the school, panting. Good. There was no one around, unless she counted the first-grader being dropped off early by his parents. All Eleanor had to do was go to the classroom, find Michael Pirkle's desk, and cram in the note. No one would know. Misty would be proud of how well she had carried off the job. Michael Pirkle would get over it.

Eleanor's heart pounded as she heaved open the heavy red door of the school. The scraping sound it made on the threshold reminded her of fingernails raking a chalkboard. She looked over her shoulder guiltily. No one was watching.

She tiptoed past the office. Mrs. Stamos, the school secretary, wasn't at her desk. On the other side of the office, last year's school yearbook was laid open on the black vinyl couch.

Eleanor inhaled deeply. Deliver the note, she told herself, and Misty will be writing in your yearbook this spring. She could see it now. Misty'd put, "To a cute and funny girl," or even better, "To an awesome secret twin." All she had to do was deliver the note. *Don't* give up, she reminded herself. *Do* be creative.

She sneaked into the empty classroom. The smell of chalk dust and musty books burned the insides of her nose. She dropped her backpack in front of Michael Pirkle's desk, and clenching her teeth, wormed her hand under her books. Her fingertips connected with toilet paper. It was cool from being on the bottom of her bag, but at least it hadn't grown.

Of course it hadn't grown! she scolded herself. It was just a long piece of toilet paper with something silly written on it.

Eleanor shoved the note under a book in Michael Pirkle's desk. Her skin made contact with something rubbery but jagged, like the end of an eraser if someone had bitten—

Eleanor jerked back. The landslide began.

It was awful. In an avalanche of papers, books crashed to the floor. Michael's social studies book, his science book, his health book—each landed like a clap of thunder. Papers wafted down in the aftermath, fallout from the explosion.

Eleanor crouched by the desk. She was sure to be caught now. How would she explain? Could she say she had lost something in Michael Pirkle's desk? That she mistakenly thought Michael's desk was hers? That she had just been walking by and all his books started falling to the floor? As Eleanor groped for excuses, a final folder slid out on top of the whole incriminating heap.

The folder was baby blue, with a sad-eyed puppy holding up its paw on the front. It was the kind of puppy you'd see at a pound and immediately want to adopt. Its eyes begged for love.

Eleanor stared at the folder, something hard and sore growing in her stomach. She knew that face. She had seen those eyes.

They were the eyes of Michael Pirkle.

The only thing left in Michael Pirkle's desk besides his chewed-up erasers was the toilet paper note. Eleanor scooped it up and stuffed it in her pocket.

The lights switched on.

"Eleanor!"

Eleanor whirled around, her heart crashing against her ribs.

Mrs. Leto!

Mrs. Leto shut the door and strode over to her desk at the front of the room. She smiled at Eleanor as she hoisted a large canvas bag full of books onto her desk. "What brings you in so early this morning? This must be a first."

Eleanor glanced guiltily at the pile of books in front

of Michael Pirkle's desk. Her mind groped frantically for an acceptable reason to be in the classroom. She'd forgotten her homework? She wanted to come early to study? She didn't realize what time it was? The toilet paper note smoldered in her jeans pocket like a charcoal briquette.

As if tipped off by Eleanor's guilty brain waves, Mrs. Leto's gaze wandered over to Michael Pirkle's books. Instantly, she locked her arms across her chest. One corner of her mouth curled up in disgust.

"Somebody's in trouble!"

Eleanor could feel her knees shaking. Guilt and shame washed over her, one after the other. Okay! her mind protested. So I almost did something cruel and stupid! So I almost gave Michael a love note, just to please a friend I'm not so sure likes me! Is it so bad to want to be liked? Is that such a crime?

Mrs. Leto shook her head. "This is the third time this week I've come in here and found Michael's books all over the floor. I've told him, 'Michael, clean out your desk. It's just too full,' but does he—"

Eleanor interrupted. "The *third time?*"

"Yes." Mrs. Leto peered at Eleanor. "Why?"

Was it possible? Did Mrs. Leto not suspect . . . ? Eleanor shook her head. "Nothing."

Mrs. Leto turned to her canvas bag and started pulling out books and papers. "Would you mind picking up Michael's books for me, Eleanor? I'm afraid someone will trip over them."

"Sure!" Eleanor knelt by Michael's desk and enthusiastically began stuffing things inside. This must be the beginning of good luck, she told herself. She'd put the whole love note thing behind her and start out fresh. If Misty wanted to be her friend, Misty would just have to accept things her way. Starting with secret twins. No more sneaking. Or winking. If they were really buddies, Misty could just—

The door swung open. Misty and Jessica clattered into the room. Eleanor froze behind Michael's desk, the puppy-dog folder red-hot in her hand. Her bravery crumbled like chalk dust.

Jessica spotted her first. "What are you doing in here, Hope?"

"Eleanor's helping me get ready for the onslaught," Mrs. Leto replied matter-of-factly. "You girls can help, too. Will you put one of these papers on each desk, Jessica? Misty, you can put these folders in the 'Work In' basket."

Eleanor glanced at Misty. Misty was staring at the puppy-dog folder. A knowing smile was spreading across her face.

Jessica snatched the papers from Mrs. Leto's desk. "I don't know why Misty had to get here so early," she grumbled.

Cramming things into Michael's desk, Eleanor could

feel Misty's gaze boring a hole in her back. She knew why Misty had come early. Misty wanted to check on Michael's note.

There were footsteps in the hall. Rachel! Eleanor thought in a flash of hopefulness. The steps drew nearer, passing the drinking fountain, the rest rooms, Mr. Mandock's room. The door of Mrs. Leto's classroom slammed against the wall. Michael Pirkle ricocheted into the room.

Across the room, Misty laughed. Panic rose like steam from Eleanor's neck.

Mrs. Leto strode over and took Michael by the shoulders. "Good morning, Michael! You're just who we were looking for!" She propelled Michael toward his desk. "Eleanor's started something that you should have finished long ago. Say, 'Thank you, Eleanor.'"

"Thank you, Eleanor," Michael mumbled.

There was a meaningful snort from across the room.

Head down, Eleanor shuffled over to her own desk. In two minutes, Misty would realize that Michael didn't have the note. In two minutes, Misty would be furious. Two little minutes, and her brief career as a secret twin would be finished. She realized now that Misty wasn't much of a twin, but did it have to end so fast? At this rate, she'd be a candidate for the *Guinness Book of World Records*: "Shortest Attempt at Popularity—Eleanor Cotton, Atlanta, Georgia. Age 12."

Michael retrieved the wastepaper basket from underneath the pencil sharpener and began throwing papers directly into the trash. Nick, Theo, and some other boys strayed into the room. Jessica stole Theo's math book. Theo started chasing her. Nick sharpened a pencil. Misty brushed her hair.

Eleanor buried her head in her arms. It was just a matter of time.

"Psssst, Michael."

Eleanor bolted upright. Misty was leaning over Michael.

Misty flung back her hair. "Michael," she said sweetly, "you finding anything interesting in there?"

Michael squinted up at Misty. He pointed to himself.

Misty smiled reassuringly. "Yes, Michael. You. Did you find anything, ah, interesting?"

Michael scratched his head. "Well, I did find an Endangered Animals of the World card I thought I'd lost. Siberian tiger." He held up a card.

Misty frowned. "No, Michael. I mean like"—she lowered her voice—"like something you'd use in the *bathroom.*"

Eleanor cringed.

"No-ooo . . ."

Misty whispered something in his ear.

Michael jerked back. *"Toilet paper?"* he exclaimed.

Jessica and Theo quit running. Nick stopped sharpening his pencil. The classroom got unnaturally silent.

Misty put her finger to her lips, but it was too late.

"Misty," Nick said, "if you have to go, the bathroom is two doors down."

Misty's skin turned a delicate pink. "Oh, Michael, it was only a joke." She tried to laugh.

"What joke? What toilet paper?" Jessica demanded. She turned toward Eleanor, her eyes tiny slits. "Hope, why do I get this feeling this has something to do with you?"

"Jessica," Misty said brightly, "will you go with me to the drinking fountain?"

Jessica jammed her hands on her hips. "I'm not moving until Eleanor tells me what you and her were up to." Behind Jessica's back, Misty shook her head quickly. There was fear in her eyes, a fear, Eleanor knew with sudden clarity, that she wanted no part of.

Something lifted inside of Eleanor. It was as if a giant clamp had been removed from her heart. None of the old things mattered anymore. Being Misty's friend, keeping Jessica happy, being liked—none of it mattered. She felt as light and feathery as a pencil shaving.

She smiled before she said it.

"Oh, Jessica, just stuff it!"

Over in the doorway, Rachel clapped.

⟦ 21 ⟧
Into the Past

"By the way, Eleanor," said Rachel, holding the blackberry bush upright in her bike basket with one hand as she steered her bike with the other, "you owe us two dollars and eight cents, since you forgot to bring it to school."

Eleanor nodded solemnly. That wasn't all she had forgotten. She had been so upset about delivering the toilet paper note that morning that she hadn't remembered to ride her bike to school, either. She had to ride to Green's Nursery and back with Charlie.

Eleanor held on to Charlie's waist, feeling his body shift from side to side while he pedaled standing up. When he drove through a puddle left by the morning rain, drops of dirty water sprayed up from his rear tire, landing on Eleanor's hair and back.

"Cool the puddles," Rachel said to Charlie. "You're getting Eleanor all wet."

"Sorry," grunted Charlie. He had spoken only in one-word sentences all afternoon. He wobbled his bike away from the curb.

Eleanor sighed. A little dirty water was the last thing she was worried about. If only Charlie would talk to her. Just when she was starting to like him, well . . . a lot, he wasn't speaking to her. What had she done wrong?

Rachel yelled, "Race you to the pond!"

Eleanor craned her neck to see around Charlie. Tyler Drive, in sight at last. She leaned back, fighting off the urge to lay her cheek against Charlie's jacket as his bike sped next to Rachel's, his tires smacking like kisses against the wet pavement.

Charlie stopped the bike at the pond. Without a word, Eleanor hopped off and stumbled toward the oak tree.

Rachel left her bike in the wet grass by the pond and caught up with Eleanor. "I've been meaning to ask you all day." She glanced over her shoulder at Charlie, who was struggling up the hill with his bike. "I didn't want to say anything in front of anybody—what made you tell Jessica to stuff it this morning?"

Eleanor's cheeks lit up in embarrassment. "Oh, she'd just pushed me too far, I guess. Misty and I were supposed to be secret—" Eleanor broke off. It seemed so obviously ridiculous, now.

"—twins?" finished Rachel.

143

Eleanor gasped. "How did you know?"

Rachel just laughed. "I was secret twins with her in first grade. I think everybody's been secret twins with Misty at one time or other."

The back door opened. Mrs. Cotton waved. Rachel and Charlie waved back. "Hi, Mrs. Cotton," Rachel called.

Eleanor watched as her mother watered the chrysanthemums still blooming by the patio. It occurred to her that maybe she was the one who had been worried about having friends, not her mom. Maybe it was she herself who had been the award-winning worrywart. Maybe her mom had actually believed in her all along.

Before she could give it any more thought, Buford came streaking down the yard, leaving a trail in the wet grass.

As Charlie rubbed Buford's ears, Eleanor thought about how close she had come to throwing away good friendships for bad. It's spooky, she thought as Rachel dumped the blackberry bush out of its black plastic container into one of Buford's smaller craters, how close you can come to disaster and not even know it until it's over.

Rachel finished patting the lumps of orange dirt around the bush. She sat back on her heels and studied the plant critically.

"Puny, isn't it?"

Eleanor nodded. "Sad." She and Rachel exchanged a quick smile.

"Real sad," said Rachel.

Charlie sucked in his breath, eyeing the bush. "Well . . ."

"You know you haven't said more than two words since Eleanor got on your bike?" Rachel teased. "Eleanor's been acting funny, too . . ."

Rachel held up her hand as Eleanor and Charlie protested. "Oh, just shut your eyes, you two. Let's see if the bush worked."

Relieved to change the subject, Eleanor shut her eyes.

Immediately, the air began to thicken and hum, but jerkily, like a car straining to start. Joseph's image flickered into view, then was replaced by a bright purple light. After a moment, Eleanor realized that she was staring at the insides of her own eyelids.

"We're losing him," said Charlie, sighing.

Rachel pulled her beret down over her ears. "It's so *sad*."

Eleanor picked up an acorn and threw it toward the pond. It rolled down the hill past Buford, who snapped at it, then plunked in the water. It made a small circle of ripples in the yellow-gold reflection of the late afternoon sun. As strongly as she had once feared and loathed him, Eleanor had come to regret Joseph's passing.

After a long silence, Rachel said, "You know, in Joseph's honor, I think we should all go trick-or-treating this year as pioneers. Charlie, you can be a soldier if you—"

Just then, from up by the house, there came an awful blast. Eleanor thought wildly of wounded elephants.

Hooooonk!

All three Pretenders turned at once. Audrey was skipping down the hill. She waved a black and dented horn in the air, and then put it to her lips.

Hooooonk!

Buford bounded up to Audrey and began nipping at her arms. Audrey held the horn over her head.

"Au-drey!" Eleanor demanded. "What *is* that?"

Audrey beamed. "Like it? It's a real Silver War bugle. Told you Tyler was giving me something good!"

Next to Eleanor, Charlie froze. "Audrey, where'd you get that?"

Audrey admired the bugle, twisting it this way and that in her hand. "From Tyler. Neat, huh?"

Charlie cleared his throat. He seemed to have a hard time breathing. "Did, uh, Tyler say where he got it?"

Audrey laughed. "That's the funny thing. He got it from my own yard! Or at least his dad did. His dad built this house, did you know that? He even named that street back there after Tyler. Tyler Drive. I wish there was an Audrey Street."

Charlie sat down heavily, right in the wet grass. "It's Joseph's bugle," he murmured. His voice was thick with wonder.

"No it's not," said Audrey. "It's Tyler's—was Tyler's. Now it's mine."

"Oh, Audrey," exclaimed Rachel, "you don't know, do you?"

"Know what?"

"Eleanor, didn't you tell her about the ghost?"

"Ghost?"

Audrey looked up at Eleanor eagerly. Eleanor was not surprised, this time, to see the cute baby Audrey shine through. Audrey had had the same expression on her face the day Eleanor taught her how to hide peas under her plate.

Tell her, something inside Eleanor said. *Audrey's not the enemy. Audrey is . . . Audrey. Cute. Dumb. Your sister.*

"A ghost lives under this tree—don't look like that, he's not scary. His name is Joseph. He's from the Ci-vil, not Silver, War."

"Ooooo, cool!"

"Don't go getting too excited about him. He's probably not going to be around much longer. We think he's losing his connection to the present."

"Huh?"

Eleanor smiled. "Its hard to explain. But what it boils down to is this—if that's Joseph's bugle Tyler gave you, and we give it back to Joseph, well, then maybe he'll stick around here longer."

"You mean you need Tyler's present?"

Eleanor sighed. She should have known Audrey wouldn't—

"Here, take it." Audrey held out the bugle.

Eleanor stared at the bugle. "Really?"

"Yep."

"*Really?*"

"We have to keep the ghost."

Eleanor felt such a powerful mixture of pride and love that she had to grit her teeth.

"Let me relieve you of that," said Rachel, prying the bugle from Audrey's fingers. She handed it to Charlie, who cradled it lovingly in his hands. Respectfully, he placed the bugle under the oak tree.

There was no need to speak. The four of them sat in a circle in the wet grass, the bugle in the middle. Eleanor's right knee accidentally touched Charlie's left knee. Charlie didn't move. She didn't either, not even after Buford flopped down behind her and nudged his nose into her back.

"Now, Audrey, you've got to close your eyes," Rachel said.

Eleanor's heart pounded. She was afraid to close her own eyes. Now that Joseph had his bugle, what would they see?

Across the circle, Audrey squeezed her eyes shut so hard that her nose wrinkled.

If Audrey could do it . . . Eleanor took a huge breath and closed her eyes.

The air hummed and thickened like never before. Eleanor's ears rang with it. Her bones ached under the pressure. She felt as though all her molecules were being squeezed into a tiny, tiny tube. She was going down, down, down, through the tunnel of time.

Suddenly, her vision exploded in the bright light of a summer's day. Before her in a thicket were dozens of young men, picking blackberries. Their frying pans and rifles clunked noisily against their blue-shirted backs. Their talk filled the air.

Eleanor heard a loud crack. Past the bushes, she caught sight of a beaver diving under the surface of a pond. Many of the men were unbuttoning their shirts and looking longingly through the brush at the water. Eleanor could understand why; dust and sweat mingled powerfully with the heat of the day.

When the boys began pulling off their boots and un-buttoning their trousers, Eleanor politely shifted her mind's-eye view to the boy under the tree. Joseph. Her Joseph. He was cradling a tin cupful of blackberries in his lap. He grinned, revealing a boyish gap between his teeth. A cowlick at his hairline made his bangs stick out. He looked all of twelve years old.

Eleanor knew he had only minutes to live.

And then, as her throat burned with tears, through the many layers of time and experience, into the present, Eleanor felt a hand. Charlie's hand, squeezing hers. It felt warm and wonderful. Solid.

Eleanor squeezed it back, and dove back into the past.